THE TUNNEL

GAYNE C. YOUNG

SEVERED PRESS
HOBART TASMANIA

THE TUNNEL

Copyright © 2019 Gayne C. Young
Copyright © 2019 by Severed Press

WWW.SEVEREDPRESS.COM

ISBN: 978-1-925840-79-7

1.

"His face looks like hamburger meat. His nose has been ripped from his face. Ears shredded off. Eyes pulled...no, gouged from their sockets. Half his fingers are gone..."

Jeff Hunter stood from the destroyed figure that lay in a dried puddle of blood upon a plastic tarp on the floor in the center of the converted barn. The air smelled of blood and death, dust, and farm machinery. "Rival cartel didn't do this. A chainsaw sure as hell couldn't have done this. This was something else."

"So, you believe him? That he and his men were attacked by...by monsters?!" Miguel scoffed in anger.

He flew across the room to the metal folding chair where Julio sat. The poor man's face was painted in dried blood and streaks of sweat and filth. He trembled in fear and in anticipation of what would surely be the torturous death that awaited him. "What did you say they were? The things that killed everyone but you? Twelve of my best diggers? Albino apes? Ghost apes?"

"Monkeys," Julio mumbled. He swallowed then offered in broken English, "They to have tails."

"Tails?! Are you being a smart ass?!" Miguel exploded.

"No, *jefe*," Julio assured Don Miguel. "No. I to promise. I just wanna...wanna to tell to you the truth."

"The truth?" Miguel countered. "You should have started with that. Trust me. Things would have been much easier if you had."

Miguel looked to the two huge *sicarios* that stood patiently against the wall. Juan and Arturo resembled NFL linebackers. Each was a mass of muscle and intimidation. They had grown up in the Acuña Cartel. It was in their blood, they'd seen and done it all, and had no problem doing such. And they enjoyed topping the previous actions of others and themselves in terms of pain and notoriety.

Juan and Arturo stepped forward then halted when Hunter raised his hand in a commanding gesture.

Hunter walked to the chair where Julio sat in terror and knelt on the sweat-stained packed earth floor before him. He looked at Julio then directed Juan to bring him a bottle of water. Juan looked to Miguel for approval and when it was given retrieved a bottle of water.

He gave it to Hunter who opened it and gave it to Julio, who drank furiously.

"When's the last time you ate?" Hunter asked.

Julio thought for a moment then replied in a frightened voice, "Yesterday."

Hunter nodded and once more looked to Juan. Miguel saw what was coming and nodded for Juan to retrieve food for the frightened man.

Hunter stood and opened a metal chair in front of Julio and sat. He leaned forward and spoke.

"Here's how I operate," Hunter began, his voice calm and direct. "I look to see what I can do to help the people I work with. And in your case, that's helping you get set up in the States. Is that right?"

"Yes." Julio nodded. "I very much want this."

"I know," Hunter assured him. "You've got a wife and two kids back in Tijuana and you took this job for Mr. Alvarado to make some money so you can get you and your family over into Texas."

Julio nodded and stuttered, "San Antonio. San Antonio is where. We have family…the relatives there."

"Good," Hunter continued, his voice calm but authoritative. "That's a fantastic dream. To give your family something better is what every man wants in life."

"Yes," Julio agreed. "I want daughters go good schools. Maybe to college one day. They very smart. Work very hard."

"Julio, I can make that happen. Actually, it's Mr. Alvarado that can make that happen. He has plenty of resources to see that your dreams become realities. All I need…"

"What you need?" Julio eagerly interrupted. "What you…what do Don Alvarado need? I promise it. I promise."

"I know," Hunter took control of the conversation once more. "I need you to tell me what happened then help me to prove that that's what actually happened."

Fear returned to Julio's face.

Hunter's easy manner had put Julio somewhat at ease but once more his head was flooded with the image of violence and pain that awaited him. His brother had gotten off easy dying the way he did. What the two *sicarios* staring at him in anger could and probably would do to him would be a far worse and a much slower death than the fate that had claimed his brother.

And the others.

Julio swallowed and asked in a timid voice, "Prove?"

Hunter shook his head. "No, the proof comes after the telling. Tell me what happened."

"I is…am," Julio stuttered in fear. Tears welled in his eyes.

"Julio, relax. Just tell me what happened. Take your time."

"I is afraid you no to believe 'cause I no can believe and I live it."

"That's fine. That's where the proof comes in. You tell me what happened then help me find a way to prove it. But that's later, okay? Now is the telling. Just start at the beginning."

Juan returned with a plate of food. He placed it on a table and Julio looked in that direction. When he caught Juan's stare, Julio lowered his head and swallowed. He wiped his eyes and gave Hunter his full attention once again.

"My brother was …he working jackhammer," Julio began.

"Your brother Ernesto, right?

"Yes. He older. He drilling the wall and it cave in. All. There was nothing on other side of rock. He fall forward. I help him up and we see that he cut into big cave. Very big."

"How big?" Hunter interrupted.

"Very," Julio promised. "Our lights no hit other side. Roof maybe three story. I and others never see nothing like it. We all stop to look inside. It smell very bad. Air is wet. We talk about what to do then…"

Tears welled forth and spilled from Julio's eyes and down his cheeks. He wiped his face and looked to what was left of his brother lying on the tarp. He looked back to Hunter and wiped his eyes again.

"Then they come," Julio promised. "White flashes. They jump on all. One jump on Ernesto. He fall back on me. I trapped underneath. It tear him apart. Screaming and yelling. I see men die and be eat."

Hunter nodded in understanding then asked, "What did they look like? The things that attacked you?"

"They white. All white. Look like…" Julio paused in thought. "I don't know English. Look like *babuino*."

"*Babuino*?" Hunter asked. He looked to Miguel for a definition.

"*Babuino* means baboon. It means baboon," Miguel scoffed in anger. "And you better get him to the proving part of this bull shit story ASAP because my patience is wearing thin. Very thin."

Hunter ignored his employer and turned back toward Julio.

"They looked like baboons? White baboons?"

"Yes."

"How'd you get away? If they were killing everyone?"

"They attack. Go back in cave. I stay under Ernesto long time. Drag him back. To bury him."

Julio wiped the tears that trailed down his face.

"Okay." Hunter nodded. "I believe you, Julio. But how do we prove this? How can you prove that everyone in that tunnel but you was killed by white baboons?"

"Ernesto kill one."

"What?" Hunter asked in disbelief.

Miguel came closer.

"Ernesto stab one with screwdriver," Julio said matter-of-factly. "It on him. He stab many times. It fall dead. Ernesto try to stand but he no get up."

"There's one of these things down there? In the tunnel? A dead one?"

"Yes."

"Baboons!" Miguel exploded. He directed his attention toward Hunter and barked, "Why are you entertaining him?"

Hunter stood. He started to speak but Miguel cut him off.

"What happened was someone tunneled in from the other side," Miguel theorized. "Thinking they could take control of what we've started. Someone from the Gulf or Baja Cartels. They've been trying to cut into our territory for years."

Hunter stood motionless.

Silent.

Miguel took these actions as disagreement on Hunter's part.

"Baboons? Really?" Miguel ridiculed. "You're smarter than that."

"Julio says there's proof," Hunter calmly stated. "Me and my team are going to have to go down there regardless to check things out…"

"When?" Miguel demanded.

"Day after tomorrow…"

"Why not today? Or tomorrow?" Miguel continued.

"This is right up my boy Taylor's alley. He saw more tunnel action in Afghanistan than anyone left alive. I want him in on this. Regardless of what's down there."

"Taylor?" Miguel asked in shock. "You've been trying to get him onboard for over a year."

"The trying part's over." Hunter smiled. "This morning, we move on to the getting part."

2.

Jarrett Taylor found it hard not to dwell on the past.

But it was almost impossible not to when you're reminded of it on a constant basis.

When every day brings letters, emails, phone calls, summons, bills, threats of lawsuits, and more to remind you of that past.

Taylor's look at his past always began with his divorce.

With visual memories of his wife of more than a decade telling him she was leaving him before he shipped out for his second tour in Afghanistan.

"You love them more than you love us! More than you love me and more than you love Avery," she'd screamed in the middle of explaining her reasons for wanting out of their marriage and life together.

What them was she talking about, Taylor wondered.

The enemy?

His men?

The people he was supposed to be aiding?

He never got an answer.

Taylor was in the middle of his third and final tour when he got the call to come home.

That his baby girl was sick.

Astrocytomas.

The doctors tried cutting it out of her.

Cut into his baby girl's brain.

But it didn't take.

She was dead in under six months.

Five months since Avery's death and he was still getting notices of failure to pay child support.

Child support.

That was a funny one.

How could you pay child support on a dead child?

And yet the notices kept coming.

So too did the notices from hospitals and collection agencies, the promises of legal action against him from those entities, and the calls from his ex-wife who constantly blamed him for all that had befallen her.

It was never-ending.

And then Hunter called.

Made his way through all the other callers to finally get to Taylor. To ask him to reconsider his offer.

To promise him financial salvation, the offer of a new life and the return to a tightknit group of friends—no, to the family—that he'd lost.

This time, Taylor agreed.

Why not?

He had nothing else in life.

Nothing that he cared about or that gave him a feeling of belonging.

Or of hope.

It was time to start over.

To begin anew.

Taylor tried to put all this out of his mind and instead focus on the day before him.

He had put what little furniture and few items of value he had in a storage unit outside of Austin then sold his truck to the owner of the facility's son. The kid was nice enough and even agreed to drive Taylor to the airport in exchange for some gas money.

The kid had tried to get Taylor to buy him some beer as well, but Taylor laughed and said that he didn't want his last act in the United States for a long time to come to be breaking the law by providing booze to a minor.

"I had to ask," the 19-year-old explained with a chuckle.

"You did," Taylor countered.

Taylor was dropped at the Austin Executive Airport at noon.

Hunter arrived in a private jet twenty minutes later.

"Look at you, you sonuva bitch!" Hunter exploded in laughter at the sight of Taylor.

Hunter shook his old friend's hand then pulled him into a bear hug and slapped him on the back. He pulled back and smiled and gave his friend the once-over.

"Looking pretty good there, Captain." Hunter laughed.

"Thank you, Colonel." Taylor smiled for the first time in a very long time.

"A little more around the middle and quite a bit of gray on the sides…"

"I could say the same of you," Taylor rebuked in jest.

Hunter continued laughing.

"Yep. That's what happens when you get as old as us." Hunter looked to the floor next to Taylor. "That all you got? One bag?"

"Do I need more?"

"You will. But we'll take care of that later. Come on. Let's get the hell outta here."

3.

Angel Lòpez thought building a border wall was one of the dumbest ideas he'd ever heard.

He gladly took the job of building it though.

Money was money after all.

His problem with the wall was that it was incomplete.

That it was only going to be built in sections.

Ten miles here.

Two miles there.

A hundred miles of no wall.

Several border lakes with no barrier between Texas and Mexico.

The fact that he and his crew were cutting roads where there had previously been nothing but thousands upon thousands of acres of impenetrable scrub brush was another factor Angel thought stupid. Why give people determined to enter the U.S. at any cost a road through nowhere to do so?

Sorry for the wall you had to climb over or tunnel under.

Here's a road to civilization to make it easier for you once you overcome that slight obstacle.

The way Angel saw it, he and his crew were providing illegals more opportunities to enter the States than they were doing anything else.

But Angel's company wasn't given a contract so Angel could offer advice on border protection.

The company was given a contract to assist in the building of the wall.

The work was dull as hell, hotter than hell, and located out in the middle of hell. Angel and his nine-man crew had to camp in the bush and only rarely drove the 110 miles back into town for supplies. They'd work this way until the 10-mile stretch of wall they were building was complete. So far, they had set only a mile of upright steel posts. It would take them another three months to complete that task alone. Who knew how long it'd take to actually set the wall after that.

Angel walked along the rocky earth that baked under the relentless Texas sun toward the excavator-mounted hydraulic jackhammer that sat idling. He looked to the operator of the machinery for indication of why the hammering had stopped but Carlos offered nothing in the way of visual explanation.

"Why'd you stop?" Angel yelled over the rock-concert-level loudness of the machinery idling in place.

Carlos tapped his ear protection in response.

Angel pulled his hand across his throat in a "cut it" motion and Carlos obliged by powering down the excavator he sat within. Angel climbed onto the treads and leaned into the open cab.

"Why'd you stop?" Angel asked again.

"Feels funny," Carlos said, gesturing to the ground before him.

"What feels funny? The hammer acting up?"

"No," Carlos replied, this time pointing at the ground. "The rock. It's different."

"So what?" Angel argued. "Punch it out."

"Telling ya, man, it feels different," Carlos explained. "Last mile's been the same hard-ass rock. This hole started the same. Three feet down it's all...just different. Feels weird."

"Rock feels different," Angel scoffed. "Who cares? Come on, man. Punch it out."

"You the boss," Carlos said, nodding.

Carlos cranked the excavator back to life and Angel jumped from the treads and walked toward the hole Carlos had started. Angel looked into the massive gash and, seeing nothing out of the ordinary, turned and walked away. He turned back when he heard the jackhammer's change in sound then watched in horror as the ground around the striking hammer gave way.

Carlos threw the excavator in reverse and gunned it back and away from the imploding earth. Angel watched in disbelief as rock and gravel, dirt and debris fell inward, leaving a Suburban-sized sinkhole.

Angel turned to Carlos and motioned for him to continue backing away from the hole. Angel's crew jumped from Bobcat track loaders, sprung from pickup beds, scrambled from the shade, and rushed to the edge of the hole. Carlos killed the excavator and rushed to join them.

"Don't get too close," Angel warned, gesturing for the men to back away.

"Told you that shit felt different," Carlos barked.

"How deep is that thing?" a worker named Antonio wondered aloud.

Marco pulled the cell phone from his pocket and used it as a flashlight to peer into the void. "Shit's deep!"

"Don't get too close," Angel warned again.

Antonio left and returned with a flashlight. He stood at the edge of the sinkhole and shined the beam downward.

"That's real deep," Antonio detailed. "Like, walk around inside of there deep."

"Yeah, we're done for the day," Carlos exclaimed.

"What?" Angel questioned.

"I ain't driving over that, some big-ass cavern," Carlos explained. "And I sure ain't gonna jackhammer into it. Start a bigger cave-in."

Angel wiped the growing sweat from his brow in thought.

Carlos was right.

Angel would have to call the company for guidance. They'd have a team of geologists and engineers come survey the area, debate what they'd found, then debate how to proceed. In the meantime, Angel and his crew would get paid to sit around and wait.

"Smells like shit down here!"

Angel returned from his thoughts to see Antonio climbing into the newly developed hole.

"Get outta there," Angel barked in fear.

"It's cool," Antonio offered. "The rocks fell like steps."

"Antonio! Get outta there," Angel directed once more. "Worker's comp won't pay on accidents involving you being a dumbass."

"Dumbass? Ha!" Antonio laughed. "I'm an explorer."

Most of the crew laughed and all watched as Antonio lowered himself further into the hole.

Antonio stepped down the jumble of rocks that led into what he discovered was a vast cavern. The rocks that had collapsed from Carlos' hammering had fallen upon a spur that grew from the cavern floor. Antonio made his way down the rocks and then to the rise and then to the floor below. He exited the beam of light that shone through the hole now some 20 feet above him and into a world of complete darkness. The air was humid and smelled of animal, animal feces, and dampness. Antonio's flashlight pierced the darkness to reveal a room the size of two soccer fields. Passages veered from this expanse in every direction. Stalactites hung from the ceiling and the floor was worn smooth from what Antonio guessed was from some kind of flooding.

"Watch out for bats," someone yelled from high above.

Antonio trained his beam on the ceiling and into the maze of stalactites that grew from it.

"Ain't no bats down here," he yelled back.

Antonio stepped forward then paused when his right foot came down on something brittle.

Something that snapped.

He lowered his flashlight to find the ground before him littered with bones.

There were bones of every size and every shape.

Some were bleached dry by time and others that still bore the flesh of the animals they had once been.

Antonio saw ribcages of small animals and the antlers of deer and the jawbones of javelina.

A sudden chill ran up his spine and he scanned the cave in every direction, looking for some cause for his sudden fear.

He thought he heard a low growl like that of an angry dog and he climbed the rise and up the rocks and out of the hole as fast as he could.

"He's back!" Carlos offered.

Antonio saw that Carlos had a beer in his hand and he reached out and took it and downed it in record time.

"Damn, man," Carlos complained. "I just popped that."

"What's down there?" Angel asked. He looked Antonio up and down then offered, "You look spooked."

Antonio dismissed this idea with a wave of his hand and said, "Ain't nothing down there but a whole lotta cave."

4.

"Everyone, this is Robert Wilson, owner of the ranch and our host for the week."

Robert nodded to Dr. Ken Cooke in thanks for his introduction then gestured for the group of a little more than a dozen college students to cease their applause. The group did as they asked and watched as the lean 65-year-old rancher held court from beneath the shade of a large mesquite tree. Despite the near hundred-degree temperature, Robert was the picture of vigor. He stood more than six feet tall, his tan skin barely wrinkled, and his jeans and long-sleeve shirt starched to rigid perfection. He removed his bleach-white straw cowboy hat in a gesture of hello to the females that gathered in the shade before him and addressed the crowd.

"I thank y'all for coming," Robert began, "'n' I hope it's not too hot for y'all."

The crowd chuckled and Ken said over the crowd, "This is a strong bunch. And ready for some serious paleontology field work."

Robert nodded and smiled.

"The TNT Ranch has been in my family for over five generations," Robert began anew. "Our livelihood for most of that time has been cattle 'n' oil. My wife and daughter brought some organic vegetables, craft soaps, and bird watching retreats into the mix few years back but still our main bread 'n' butter comes from cattle 'n' oil."

Robert paused to take in his audience's reaction then continued.

"A lot's changed down here on the border in the last 20 years. Illegals have always crossed through our ranch on their way up from the Rio Grande. Used to be just migrant workers and folks looking for better lives. Now they's coming up to bring drugs 'n' to traffic humans. Seeing what we've seen and getting no real help from the government has led the family 'n' me to make the hard decision to move on."

A few in the audience dropped their faces in sadness while others raised theirs in anger at Robert's plight.

"But I'm hoping to show folks just how special this area is before I go," Robert explained. "And to hopefully draw some high-interest money in the process. That's where y'all come in, I guess."

Most in the audience smiled or laughed at Robert's simplified explanation of their reasoning for being on the ranch.

"As the story goes, it was my great grandfather that found the tusk my family now knows came from a Columbian mammoth. He found it just inside the sinkhole…" Robert waved his hands as if searching for the right word to grasp onto. "Cave-in, drop, pitfall trap, whatever ya call it but when he brought that tusk home, there was hell to pay. His daddy apparently chafed his hide and reminded him in no uncertain terms that the area wasn't safe. He said he was lucky he didn't fall in deeper 'n' become part of history like everything else down there."

Ken clapped his hands in laughter.

"To my knowledge, no one has ever gone down further than what my great grandfather did that day," Robert continued. "Y'all will be the first 'n' I hope you find enough treasures that some museum comes calling with a check big enough for me to relocate someplace safer."

Most of the audience laughed and smiled at Robert's candor.

"Based on what I've seen, from the surface anyway," Ken interrupted, "it appears that the cave goes down at least thirty feet deeper from the first shelf and guys…it's about the biggest bone pile I've ever seen!"

"Good!" Robert exclaimed. "Hope y'all find some great stuff down there. But a word of warning…"

Ken and the others looked to one another in confusion then back to Robert for explanation.

"Not only has my family been on this ranch for five generations," Robert explained, "but so too have the folks that have worked right along my family. More so, actually. Their families have been on the place far longer than mine and one thing they've always passed down through the ages was the stories of how that hole is haunted. How it leads to Hell. How it's home to demons that take children. Monsters 'n' nightmares…"

Robert grinned from ear to ear and continued.

"I've never believed any of that Mexican voodoo 'n' ghost stories but thought I should warn y'all all the same."

Some in the crowd laughed at Robert's warning.

Others did not.

5.

"Your new clothes and supplies are being picked up as we speak," Hunter explained as he ended the call on his satellite phone. He walked to the rear of the plane and pulled two Dos Equis beers from the cooler that sat next to the lavatory. He returned to his seat next to Taylor and handed him a beer. The two men clicked bottles and offered toasts and took a long pull on their drink.

"Damn good," Taylor offered. "Thanks. And thanks for this."

Hunter looked up and down the plane then back to Taylor.

"What? The gear? Plane? Lack of a stewardess..."

"Thanks for the chance to start over," Taylor assured him.

Hunter smiled. "Glad to have you back in life my friend. Damn glad. Just wish you'd joined me two years ago."

"Two and a half years ago," Taylor corrected before shaking his head in disbelief. "Can't believe it's come to this though..."

"To what?"

"I appreciate your help," Taylor assured his friend once more. "But I never thought I'd see the day I'd agree to work..."

"For me?" Hunter laughed, trying to lighten his friend's souring mood. "You did so before, if you recall. Little thing called the United States Army."

Taylor cracked a laugh and took another long pull on his beer.

"You know what I mean..."

"The Acuña Cartel?"

"Christ, man, any cartel! Has life really beat me down so low..."

"Taylor," Hunter interrupted. "I told you. No. I promised you and promise you again. It's no different than working for any other private security force. Hell, it's damn near like working for the Army."

"No different?" Taylor scoffed. "I doubt that."

"You're right," Hunter countered. "It is different than working for the Army. We get paid an ass-load more, have less oversight..."

"Torture people. Dissolve enemies in acid..."

"I've never done anything like that," Hunter argued. "No one on my team has ever done anything like that."

Taylor gave Hunter a long stare of disbelief.

Hunter pulled on his beer and laughed.

"Those are Juan's jobs."

Taylor shook his head and tried not to laugh but did so anyway. He finished his beer then stood to collect another.

"Damn," Hunter commented. "Ya killed that fast enough."

"I've practiced a lot over the past year."

"Well, keep practicing." Hunter gestured to the cooler with his half-empty beer. "What the hell. Get me one too."

Taylor retrieved the beers and sat. Hunter took one of the beers, popped the top off on his seat's armrest, and began again.

"I lead a security detail for Miguel Alvarado who just so happens to be a high-ranking official in the Acuña Cartel. He's a businessman first and foremost. On his orders, my team and I have engaged members of the…let's say…the competition. We do not deal drugs, sell drugs, torture, go Scarface on anyone with a chainsaw…"

"Scarface anyone with a chainsaw!" Taylor laughed through a mouthful of beer.

"Nope," Hunter cracked up. "No Scarfacing."

"Really glad to hear that…"

"Trust me, Taylor," Hunter's eyes promised. "I never steered you wrong and never will."

6.

Tom watched Megan fumble with the small battery-operated air pump. It was supposed to easily lock tight into the valve of their shared air mattress, but Megan found the process anything but easy. She turned the pump on her face, closed her eyes, and let the pump blow air over her.

"I can't believe how hot it is in here," she moaned from behind her newly discovered fan.

"I told you," Tom reminded her, "that we should blow up the mattress up outside of the tent…"

"But then how do you get it in the tent," Megan barked. "'Cause the mattress won't fit through the door…"

"Front tent flap…"

"Whatever it's called!" Megan barked even louder. "Who gives a shit what it's called?! It's just so freakin' hot."

"Well, it is Texas," Tom said, laughing.

"Might as well be in Mexico," Megan complained. "As close to it as we are. I could probably spit into the country from here."

"Way to build international relations," Tom joked.

"Shut up!" Megan laughed.

Tom reached into the tent from his vantage point just outside the open front flap and pulled the mattress out. He gestured for Megan to follow and she crawled out of the tent and into the shade of the tree that sheltered their nylon home away from university. Megan stood and reluctantly turned off the pump blowing in her face and through her wavy dirty-blonde hair and put it in Tom's waiting open hand.

"Let me show you how it's done." Tom chuckled as he locked the pump into the mattress' valve.

"Just what I hoped to find at college," Megan chided. "A man working on a doctorate that will earn him almost nothing and who can blow up air mattresses."

"Paleontologists have to know how to blow up air mattress 'cause that's all they can afford," Tom played along. He turned on the pump and the queen-sized mattress slowly filled.

Megan sat in one of the two camp chairs outside their tent and fanned herself with her hands. She paused this action for a moment then wiped her brow with a lime green bandana she brought from her pocket then drank the remainder of the water bottle that sat in the chair's cup holder.

"So ya think this is the big one?" she asked Tom. "The one that gets you on the map and into a museum or teaching at a college afterward?"

"I'm hoping so," Tom admitted. He turned from Megan to test the fullness of the mattress. It was about halfway filled. "Ken said it looks like there's a whole lot of bones down there. We already know the pit holds the remains of at least one mammoth. It'd be great to find a few more."

"Whatcha think that rancher was talking about when he said the hole was haunted?"

"He didn't say it was haunted," Tom corrected. "He said the people on the ranch before his family said it was haunted. And that they passed that story down through the generations."

"Uh huh," Megan bemoaned. She hated how literal Tom could be sometimes.

"And my guess is that those people were fairly uneducated, and they made up a story to explain something they couldn't easily explain about the cave…"

"How it's filled with demons that steal kids?" Megan reminded Tom. "I don't think you'd need much of an education to explain that one. Something that lives in the cave has taken children. That sounds like an explanation to me."

"Not demons," Tom scoffed.

"Not demons. No. But something. What do you think it was?"

"We don't know if the missing children part of the story is real or not," Tom explained. "All we know is that there was a story told that warned kids to stay away from the cave…"

"A story they've been telling for, like, five generations he said…"

"That doesn't mean it's true. Or was true."

Tom tested the mattress once more and, finding it filled to his liking, turned off the air pump and removed it from the valve. He folded the mattress and shoved it into the tent.

"There we go," Tom announced.

"You're such a real man." Megan laughed. "What would I do without you?"

"Sleep on the rock-hard ground, I guess," Tom replied, chuckling.

He took his seat next to Megan and leaned in to kiss her. She playfully pushed him away saying she was too sweaty. Tom said he didn't care but Megan kept him at bay.

"So, what do you think could live in that cave?" Megan began again. "That could take kids?"

"I told you, I don't think that's—"

"Amuse me," Megan scoffed.

Tom thought for a moment then sighed and offered his thoughts.

"Back that long ago. Cougar or bear. Maybe a jaguar…"

"A jaguar?!" Megan scoffed. "In Texas?"

"Yeah," Tom assured her. "Texas has been home to lots of big cats. Prehistoric and in modern times."

Megan scanned the campsite as if looking for predators. Seeing only fellow college students setting up their campsites, she returned to Tom.

"Modern times, like, now?" Megan asked.

"Ranchers spot a jaguar every now and again over near Big Bend, but not around here. No," Tom promised. "Listen, the only danger that can come from the cave is falling in or us not finding anything worthwhile in it."

Megan smiled and Tom took it as an invitation.

"So…you wanna try out the air mattress? See how it holds up?" Tom asked.

Megan rolled her eyes and said, "God no! It's way too hot for anything like that."

7.

Hunter spent the last 20 minutes of the short flight from Austin to El Paso detailing the massacre in the tunnel to Taylor. Hunter explained the facts as he knew them. Thirteen Mexican laborers had been digging a tunnel large enough to drive a truck and trailer through from a nondescript ranch house in Mexico toward a nondescript ranch house in Texas. The tunnel was sparse with minimal supports, an unpaved road, and a string of lights that hung from the bare ceiling above. The crew worked slave labor hours for little pay but still took great pride in their work and did so diligently. During their relatively short time underground, the crew had dug a mile and a half of tunnel and only had another three-quarters of a mile before they would hit the Texas ranch that would serve as the exit point. A hundred or so yards past the Rio Grande and into the United States, the crew cut into a large cavern. Shortly thereafter, they were attacked by someone.

Or something.

Twelve of the 13 laborers were killed.

"I've only seen one of the bodies," Hunter explained. "And it was torn to hell. I tell you, I've never seen anything like it."

Taylor's stare demanded more details

"Guy looked like he been through a meat grinder. Ears pulled off. His eyes gouged out of their sockets and his nose and most of his fingers gone."

Taylor furrowed his brow in question.

"You said pulled off, like with rope or pliers?"

"No. They look like someone went at them with a dammed cheese grater. Just went to town until they were all shredded off."

Taylor shook his head in disgust. He had seen the evil that men could do in Afghanistan. He had encountered children as young as eight that had been gang-raped, men and women branded on their faces or carved beyond recognition for crimes against their religion, and others interrogated by having the soles of their feet beaten with sticks or pipes or removed completely. They were scenes that haunted him to this day, and he couldn't imagine how what Hunter was describing could be worse.

"My boss thinks it was a rival cartel or gang," Hunter continued. "That they tunneled in from the opposite side and ambushed our boys."

"What do you think?"

"I don't buy any of it," Hunter admitted. "The only survivor is a fella named Julio. He said what they cut into was a huge cave a couple of soccer fields large. Plus, I don't think the wounds on the body I saw were caused by a blade or a chainsaw even."

"So, he wasn't Scarfaced?" Taylor joked, trying not to laugh.

"Nope." Hunter joined in on the joke. "No Scarfacing."

Taylor killed the remainder of his beer and stood to toss the bottle in the trash. Hunter finished his beer and handed it to Taylor.

"So what do you think happened?" Taylor asked, returning to his seat. "If not a band of rivals?"

Hunter ran his hands over his face and then threw his short-cropped hair. He started to speak then paused then began again.

"Julio said it was monkeys."

"Monkeys!" Taylor scoffed.

"Monkeys," Hunter assured Taylor. "Well, baboons actually."

"I freakin' hate monkeys...Wait a minute, you don't believe this guy, do you? That there's monkeys down there?"

"Julio says his brother killed one," Hunter offered. "That its body is down there along with the digging crew."

Taylor rolled his eyes and shook his head. "Again, you believe him?"

"We'll find out tomorrow when we head down there."

8.

Hunter and Taylor were met at the airport by José Luis, a man who Hunter explained served as his, "Quartermaster, logistics expert, driver, and all around go-for."

Following introductions, José took Taylor's single carry-on bag and placed it in the rear of the late-model, nondescript Suburban. He then pulled one of several bags from the front seat and asked Taylor in broken English, "You want change?"

"Might as well," Hunter offered. "And I'd rather you made sure everything is right before we drive across the border."

Taylor agreed and the three men loaded into the Suburban. José drove from the runway to the private airport's main lodge. Taylor exited the vehicle, entered the building, and made his way to the men's room. He disrobed and put on his new clothing.

It had been a long time since he bought clothing for himself and he was pleasantly surprised that the sizes he'd given to José through Hunter had been correct. Everything Taylor put on fit him to a T. His coyote-brown tactical pants were long enough—not always an easy task given his 6'2" height—his boots were snug yet didn't rub anywhere they shouldn't, and his black shooter's shirt put function over fashion. The only problem with the clothes had nothing to do with their style or fit but what they had to fit over. Taylor's stomach had grown, albeit slightly, since his exiting the military. He thought back to Hunter's mention that they had both gone soft around the middle and he immediately countered this with a thought of his own.

Not too bad for a guy in his mid-40s.

Taylor gathered the clothing he changed from and all the bags and tags and made his way back to the Suburban.

"Don't you look nice?" Hunter laughed. "Your mom get you some new school clothes?"

"Not my mom. Your mom," Taylor cracked. "And it wasn't even my birthday. Go figure."

José laughed at the joke and Taylor took note that Hunter's quartermaster perhaps understood more English than he could speak.

Or let on.

"Appreciate the clothes, but where're my weapons?" Taylor began again.

"I have," José declared from behind the wheel. "They wait for you."

"We already had most of what you requested," Hunter offered. "What José picked up for you today with sent across the border via other channels. You can't just drive guns and ammunition into Mexico, you know. Well, we can, but it's easier not too. Boss has plenty of Border Patrol on the payroll but likes to save their services of looking the other way for more important situations."

"Why are we driving into Mexico, by the way?" Taylor asked. "Why didn't we fly direct?"

"The plane is owned by one of the companies our employer owns. We're pretty sure it's clear but with the DEA, you never know. The last thing Miguel needs is for any agency to follow us to the tunnel."

"What about this truck? Can't they follow it?" Taylor inquired.

"I steal this morning," José boasted. "We change again when we cross."

"Well, there you go," Taylor mused aloud. "Problem solved."

9.

José drove Hunter and Taylor across the bridge and into the city of Juárez, Mexico. Unlike the spacious urban sprawl of El Paso, Juárez was a city seemingly shoved together haphazardly. Its streets were narrow, its buildings sandwiched together and on top of one another, and its pedestrians sardined shoulder to shoulder upon the street. The usually heavy traffic was even more so, and it took José 20 minutes longer than he anticipated to reach the two-story parking garage where the three men would change vehicles.

José pulled the Suburban next to a khaki-colored Chevy Tahoe outfitted for ranch work with oversized tires, a brush guard, and a winch. He exited the Suburban first then nodded for Hunter and Taylor to follow. The men exited and Taylor stood silently, watching José transfer the bags from the Suburban to the Tahoe. As Taylor watched, he made note of his surroundings. The garage was decades old, crumbling in upon itself, and it reeked of stale urine and vomit. A rat sat eating some kind of food material near a crack in the outer wall and pigeons drank from a puddle on the ground next to the entrance.

"I promised you." Hunter laughed and slapped Taylor on the back. "Only the best for you."

Taylor's response was interrupted by José calling for him and Hunter to join him at the rear of the Tahoe. Taylor and Hunter walked to the back of the vehicle and watched as José opened the medium-sized Pelican case that sat inside the cargo bay.

"The fun stuff's at the ranch," Hunter offered. "But this will get you started."

José took a holstered Sig Sauer 9mm P320 pistol from the case and handed it to Taylor. Taylor removed the pistol from its nylon home, checked it for fit, and insured that it was loaded. He put the holstered pistol on the right side of his belt then took from José two double pistol magazine pouches. Taylor checked each magazine to ensure that they too were loaded then attached them to his belt as well.

"Knife? Taylor asked.

José handed Taylor a SOG fixed blade knife and sheath. Taylor affixed this horizontally to the back of his belt then turned to take the envelope that Hunter held out before him. Taylor took the envelope and opened it.

"Mexican passport, ID, and firearm license," Hunter explained.

Taylor nodded and put the contents of the envelope into his front shirt pocket.

Hunter pulled a small pistol from the inside front of his pants and handed it to José who in turn handed Hunter a rig similar to the one Taylor had just assembled on his person. Hunter put the belt containing his holstered Glock 19, ammo, and Leatherman multi-tool on, and moved toward the front passenger-side door of the Tahoe.

"Come on," Hunter instructed. "Christmas is over. Time to get to work."

José drove Taylor and Hunter through the city then east on Highway 2. The road skirted the Rio Grande and the men passed large agricultural fields of vibrant green and dotted with laborers. These gave way to smaller ranches and to a landscape of scrub brush and of mountains of weathered rock painted with a tapestry of cactus and a myriad of thorned plants. They drove through this for two and a half hours before they turned south on a single-lane dirt road. They passed through an open gate and over a cattle guard, continuing south for another hour until they came to a small ranch compound. It consisted of a half a dozen buildings circled by the remnants of pecan trees that had long since died from a lack of watering. José parked the Tahoe in front of a large barn constructed of old weathered wood and rusted corrugated tin. The three men exited the vehicle and Hunter led Taylor into the barn.

Taylor's mindset changed when he entered the building. The trip thus far had been relaxing and one of relief and rebirth. He'd put aside most of his old life and resigned himself to starting a new one. A life that would return him a world of never-ending training and monotony sprinkled with periodic episodes of inhuman violence. He entered the building prepared for such and took note of his immediate surroundings.

The building appeared to have once been a large barn or hanger of some sort. The huge open space had a packed earth floor and held a truck and cattle trailer, a cache of shovels, picks, pry bars, and other handheld digging instruments, wheelbarrows, and a flatbed trailer piled high with dirt and rock. At the far end of the barn was a ramp that led downward and toward a closed garage door. Office doors lined the left wall and the air within the building smelled of loam, diesel fuel, and carried with it the faint hint of blood and rot.

An office door opened, and a tall, thin, corporate-looking man exited. He waved to Hunter and called him over. Hunter led Taylor across the expansive floor and to the entrance of what Taylor could now see was an empty conference room.

"Productive trip, I hope," the man offered to Hunter as they shook hands.

"Very productive," Hunter replied, turning his gaze back to Taylor. "I got what I went to get."

The man smiled at Hunter then held out his hand to Taylor. The men shook hands and sized each other up.

"Captain Taylor," the man offered, still grasping Taylor's hand. "I am Eduardo León. I handle Human Resources for Señor Alvarado."

"Human Resources?" Taylor questioned in disbelief. "The Acuña Cartel has a Human Resources department?"

"Our branch does, yes," Eduardo said stoically. "One of the best. In fact…"

"I didn't mean any disrespect…" Taylor interrupted. "It's just…"

"I understand," Eduardo insisted. He nodded to Taylor then invited him into the conference room with a wave of his hand.

Taylor entered the room and was followed by Eduardo and then Hunter. The office was spacious but sparse. It had a cement floor and contained large conference table that held what Taylor assumed was Eduardo's workstation. Hunter closed the door behind them, and Eduardo took a seat behind two large computer monitors.

"Where's Alvarado?" Hunter asked as he took a seat across the table from Eduardo.

Taylor took a seat in the chair adjacent to Hunter's.

"Señor Alvarado will be here shortly," Eduardo stated. "He looks forward to meeting to Captain Taylor and to hearing of your plan to get the tunnel construction back on track."

"Call me Taylor," Taylor insisted.

"As you wish," Eduardo politely replied as he turned one of the screens around to face Taylor and Hunter. "Taylor, I've taken the liberty of opening an account for you at the same Swiss bank Hunter and the rest of his team use. I assume that will be alright with you?"

Taylor looked at Hunter in disbelief then muttered, "Sure."

"Then I'll need your electronic signature here," Eduardo said, sliding a small electronic tablet in-between the two monitors and toward Taylor. "Your paycheck will be deposited the first of every month. Your insurance went into effect this morning. Would you like your signing bonus in cash, deposited into your account, or a combination of both?"

"Signing bonus? You're kidding." Taylor almost laughed in disbelief.

"Of course you get a signing bonus. And a very nice one at that as Colonel Hunter here tells me you're worth the cost."

Taylor turned in his seat to see a man in black slacks and a heavily starched white shirt enter the room. He was sided by two much larger men who wore ill-fitting pants and guayabera shirts. Eduardo and Hunter stood, and Taylor followed suit. The well-dressed man stepped forward and held his hand to Taylor.

"Miguel Alvarado," he offered. "It is very nice to have you on board."

"Thank you for having me, Señor Alvarado," Taylor replied. "I look forward to getting to work."

"Yes," Miguel said. He sat at the table and directed Juan and Arturo out of the office with his eyes. The men left and Taylor, Hunter, and Eduardo returned to their seats. "I wish your arrival fell on better circumstances. And that you had time to acclimate to your position within the organization. Unfortunately, you'll not have that luxury."

"Understood," Taylor agreed.

"I need you and Hunter to solve this setback as quickly as possible," Miguel continued. "Discover the identity of our attackers and take the appropriate action."

Taylor listened intently to Miguel and studied him even more so. He sounded like a politician. He couldn't just come and say what he wanted. He had to talk around the issue. And despite his careful choice in words, Taylor could tell Miguel was raging inside.

That he was furious over this setback and that he felt it somehow painted him in a negative picture.

Was he always like this? So, reserved?

Or was this a show for just for him?

"The problem will be identified and eliminated," Hunter promised.

"I would hope so," Miguel stated. "I'm counting on you and your team."

10.

Ernesto's body mirrored that of the jackhammer he was operating. It was as if a man and machine were one. Both reverberated in a frenzied repetitive motion and in an attempt to control the power that surged through them.

Julio paused from shoveling the loose rock and dirt that his older brother's actions were sending everywhere to watch Ernesto work. Ernesto saw this and paused for a break.

"What you smiling at?" Ernesto asked his brother in his native tongue.

"Your gut," Julio said, laughing. "It's bouncing all around."

Ernesto rubbed his girth and laughed. "I'm in training. I want to look like a typical American, so I fit in when we get there."

"You mean a fat American."

"Yeah. Like I said, a typical American."

The two men laughed for a moment then Ernesto raised the heavy jackhammer and worked at the wall before him. Shards of rock splintered and flew in every direction, and clouds of earth and dust washed in the dim light of the cave. The percussion of the hammer was deafening and echoed throughout the tunnel. Ernesto felt a sudden give and tried to pull back, but the momentum of the hammering was too great. The wall gave way and collapsed, revealing a hole half the size of a doorway. Ernesto struggled to control the cumbersome jackhammer but was unable to do so and fell forward through the newly developed opening.

Julio watched in disbelief and horror as his brother shot forward. He rushed to Ernesto's side and helped him to his feet.

"You okay?" Julio asked in genuine fear, hoping that his brother was harmed.

"I'm fine," Ernesto said, brushing the dirt from his clothing with furious slaps of his hands.

"You sure?"

"Yeah. Yeah. I'm fine," Ernesto scoffed in embarrassment at his tumble.

The realization of where they were suddenly struck the two men and they stared into the darkness in disbelief and wonder. A narrow beam of light from the tunnel cut through the darkness to illuminate a floor of slick rock and the hint that it extended to the horizon. Workers from the tunnel ceased their duties and rushed to stand at Ernesto's and

Julio's side to see for themselves the alien world Ernesto had inadvertently gained access to.

A worker named Gio took a cell phone from his pocket and shined the light into the darkness was a little effect.

"Here," another worker scoffed, pulled a flashlight from his belt, and shined its light outward and into the void.

"Doesn't even hit the other side," the flashlight bearer exclaimed.

"If there is another side," another pondered aloud.

The flashlight trained upward and the men gazed in amazement.

"Must be three or four stories tall," Ernesto exclaimed.

"At least," Julio agreed.

"Smells like a sewer in here," another worker exclaimed.

"This ain't a sewer," the man with the cell phone countered.

"I didn't say it was a sewer. Said it smells like one. Smells like shit in here."

"Like a barnyard," another added. "Like wet dog and goat piss."

"And wet," another worker added. "Humid. Real humid."

"Be quiet!" Ernesto suddenly commanded. "Listen."

"What?" the flashlight bearer asked in a whisper. "What is it?"

"Heard something," Ernesto whispered in response. "Something like a dog growling or something."

"A dog?" Julio asked in hushed tones. "Down here?"

"Hush!" Ernesto curtly instructed. "Be still."

The men stood in the cleave of light produced by the tunnel, staring into the void and listening. Soft murmurs reminiscent of puppies crawling with unopened eyes toward their mother in search of nourishment whispered from the darkness.

The murmurs grew louder.

The flashlight beam swung to and fro, searching for their source.

"What's that?" Julio asked in a tone just above a whisper.

The murmurs became barks.

Low, deep barks.

The barks grew in volume, hardened in anger, and echoed across the measureless cavern.

Men breathed heavily.

Sweated in nervousness.

And fought to control their unease.

The cave exploded in a cacophony of howls and barks, spattered with the cackling of hyenas, the pain of mongrel curs, and the screams of someplace primordial.

The flashlight caught jade-colored reflections in the sea of blackness.

Then flashes of ivory fur.

Of clacking maws filled with teeth.

Of rage charging forward.

Someone screamed and the men scrambled toward the tunnel in panic.

The doorway to the tunnel became a melee of violence.

Men fought to move forward.

To escape.

To keep the unseen from them.

And to seal their sudden wounds.

The air was a torrent of screams and splattering blood.

Fangs and claws pierced and sliced.

Men wept in horror and in pain.

Extremities were shredded.

Viscera spilled.

God was begged for mercy.

Julio was in front of the violence, the tunnel before him an avenue to salvation.

Ernesto emitted a bloodcurdling howl.

Julio turned and rushed to his older brother.

A white blur of violence shot toward Ernesto's chest. It knocked him backward and into Julio and the two men crashed to the floor of the cave. Julio gasped as the air was forced from his lungs and he fought to get out from under the heavy weight of his brother.

Julio felt a sudden slam as if he had been hit in the chest by a sledgehammer. Ernesto screamed and writhed in the frenzy of a seizure. Blood poured from his body and onto his brother beneath him. Julio scratched and fought to move but the undulating weight pushing down on him was too great. He screamed with all the force he could muster.

He awoke to see Hunter and another Anglo looking down at him.

"Wake up, Julio," Hunter commanded. "It's time to tell my friend here all you know."

11.

Carlos exited the Porta Potty in a furious mood.

"What the hell is wrong with you guys?!" he called across the haze of dusk to the campfire where his nine coworkers sat. "That thing is nasty enough without y'all not tossing your paper down the shitter or leaving the lid open. All that just attracts flies and it's bad enough taking a crap in a hot house without a swarm of flies descending down on you!"

The men laughed at Carlos' complaints and watched in anticipation of his rant continuing.

Mario held out a joint for Carlos then pulled it from him and laughed, "Are your hands clean?"

Carlos ran his hands down Mario's face and cackled, "You tell me!"

The men exploded in laughter and Carlos ripped the joint from Mario's hand and took a long toke.

"Are my hands clean?" Carlos mocked. "Asshole."

Carlos sat next to Mario and handed him back the joint. The laughter died after a time and the men sat silently staring at the fire, watching as the last light of day faded into darkness. The joint was passed around from man-to-man as well was a bottle of cheap tequila and several tall boys of even cheaper beer. All sat contently happy in the moment except for Antonio whose stare was more of a case of worry and concern. Angel saw this and tried to pass him the tequila. Angel passed on the offer with a small gesture of his hand.

"What's wrong with you tonight?" Angel asked with fatherly concern.

"Ain't nothing wrong," Bartoli interrupted. "We got paid to do nothing but wait for most of the day. We got good herb and drink. No wives or girlfriends around to bitch and moan. Life is good!"

The men laughed and when the joy died down, Antonio detailed what was wrong.

"I'm just tired, I guess," Antonio confessed.

"You ain't tired," Mario stated through the firelight. "You're scared."

"Scared of what?" Antonio asked.

"You've been scared ever since you climbed out of that hole," Mario declared as he gestured over his shoulder in the direction of the cave in the construction caused earlier in the day.

"Yeah," Carlos agreed. "You've been all kind of weird since you went down there. You see a ghost down there or something?"

"No, it was scarier than a ghost," Mario said, laughing. "He saw that gal he knocked up down in Piedras Negras down there. She had his kid on her arm and a hand out looking for money."

All but Antonio cackled in laughter.

"There weren't anything down there to see," Antonio snapped. "Just a bunch of old bones."

"So, you're scared of bones?" Carlos said.

"Y'all need to lay off the drugs," Antonio commanded. "You're all acting crazy. I told you I wasn't scared. Not scared now. There's nothing down there."

The men chuckled at Antonio's mood and passed the marijuana, liquor, and beer to one another. Antonio stood from his folding chair and intercepted the bottle of tequila going around. He took a long pull and put the bottle back in rotation. He walked from the fire and away from the jokes and the chatter and into the darkness. He made his way past his hammock that hung between two mesquite trees and toward the construction equipment that stood idle in the starlight. He made his way to the edge of the cave-in and stood staring downward into the dark abyss. He unzipped his pants and began urinating into the darkness below.

"Didn't nothing down there scare me," Antonio told himself aloud. "Not a damn thing. That was just the wind or something I heard."

Antonio listened to his urine stream hit the rocks below and looked to the star-filled sky above. The tranquility of the place was suddenly interrupted by faint chattering.

Of a sound reminiscent of castanets.

Antonio scanned the horizon for the source of the intrusive sound. His gaze turned downward and into the hole he was still urinating into. A blaze of motion shot from the hole. Antonio was knocked upward and back. He slammed to the ground and instinctively threw out his hands to hold the terror on top of him at bay.

Antonio screamed as a muzzle of glistening canines thrust forward. His nose was ripped from his face with a blinding shock of pain. Blood and tears poured over his cheeks, into his mouth, and down his neck. He howled in anguish then shrieked as four fingers were bit from his left hand. He wrestled to free himself from the terror, but the beast's strength and tenacity was too great. He focused the last of his strength into a scream for help, but it was ripped from his throat by the jaws atop him.

12.

"What the hell was that?" Angel asked in a visible state of shock.

The scream he and the others around the campfire heard was bloodcurdling.

Terrifying.

Primal.

From someone or something in the last grasp of life.

Angel stood and the others followed.

"Was that... Antonio?" Carlos wondered aloud.

"Shit ain't funny if it was," Mario stated.

"Sure as hell didn't sound like he was joking to me," Carlos continued. "Sounded like...like... Hell, I don't know what it sounded like...."

Carlos trailed off, not wanting to share what evil scenarios were flashing through his head.

Angel pulled a flashlight from his pocket and turned it on. He walked toward the screams and the others followed. Carlos and Mario turned on their flashlights and made their way to the front of the group.

The group marched cautiously past the campsite where their hammocks hung and toward the wide clearing they carved had through the scrub with bulldozers and backhoes in the days previous. Their lights panned over the construction equipment and into the open cabs of each, looking for Antonio.

"Sounded like he was over this way," Angel clarified.

"Where's that cave-in?" Bartoli asked. "Maybe he fell in."

"Hole's over..." Angels voice went stone dead at the scene his flashlight illuminated.

Three white animals stood feeding on what was left of Antonio's body. The lead creature raised its head and bared blood-soaked fangs. It growled in warning and the other beasts bared their canines that glistened with blood and viscera. The lead animal charged forward and the men turned in unison and ran in the direction of the campfire.

The scrub brush turned into a maelstrom of violence, of flashlight beams strobing the darkness, of screams and cries, of barks and howls, of men cut down and opened with teeth and claws, and of animalistic strength over human frailty.

13.

"No, no, no." Jared laughed in drunken euphoria. He was 11 Lone Star Lights into the evening and feeling rather intelligent and felt that challenging his professor in front of his classmates was the best way to prove such. "Chupacabras are real."

Dr. Cooke laughed across the campfire. "They're a myth. No different than Bigfoot or the Loch Ness Monster."

"Okay. Back up," Jared suggested with a laugh. "Bigfoot is more likely than not to be an actual animal but has yet to be proven. The Loch Ness Monster is total bullshit. But chupacabras are real and that my good doctor is 100% true."

"What's a chupa…cupa…chalupa?"

The students drinking around the campfire exploded into laughter at Angie's question.

"A chalupa's like an open-faced taco," Aubrey explained to her roommate. "A chupacabra is a Tex-Mex myth. It's like a kangaroo-looking thing that sucks the blood out of goats. Kind of like a vampire."

"And according to Jared, they're real," Dr. Cooke said with a chuckle.

"If you will allow," Jared slurred as he stumbled out of his camp chair. "Yes, the chupacabra is said to resemble a kangaroo or a baboon absent a tail comes from a myth—yes, a myth—born in Puerto Rico that made its way here to the Tex-Mex Border. The real chupacabra…"

Jared paused to burp.

"Here we go," a grad student from Harlingen named Hope scoffed.

"Excuse me," Jared began again. "The real chupacabra is a hairless coyote. Some say it suffers from mange. Others that it's a genetic anomaly and others that they are bred that way on some secret ranch. They are found throughout South Texas and make the news every now and again when some rancher or hunter shoots one. They were named 'chupacabra' by the press and it has become the official name for this animal."

"I've seen that!" Dr. Cooke joyfully announced. "On the news. Is that really what they're calling those hairless things? Chupacabras?"

"Yes, sir, that they are," Jared said. He fell back into a camp chair and killed the beer that sat at his feet.

"Well, then, I stand corrected, Jared," Dr. Cooke announced. "Thanks for enlightening me and anyone else that didn't know that."

"You are welcome," Jared said just before vomiting.

14.

"I can't believe Jared puked in front of everyone," Tom said in disbelief. "In front of Dr. Cooke. I mean, that's Jared's doctorate advisor."

"Yep. He's an idiot," Megan agreed.

Tom rolled over to face Megan in the half darkness. Her face was cast in the soft light of the stars that filtered through the open mesh roof of their tent. She was beautiful.

"Quit looking at me like that," Megan said, giggling.

"Like what?" Tom asked, trying to be coy.

"Like you want to do me."

"I always want to do you."

"I'm sooooo flattered but we're out here in the woods, it's 90° at 11 o'clock at night, and I smell like absolute shit. It ain't happening."

Tom smiled then leaned in to kiss Megan again anyway. She received his affection then pushed him away and joyfully warned, "Don't get too excited there, chief. I'm telling you, it ain't going to happen. Not 'til I get back home to a shower and some A/C."

Tom smiled and stared up at the sky through the mesh roof of tent. He lay there, enjoying the moment until Megan spoke again.

"Is it true, what Jared said?"

Tom rolled over to once again face Megan.

"Is what true?" he asked.

"That those hairless chupacabra things are out here."

"I don't know," Tom admitted.

"You don't know," Megan mocked in an over-exaggerated impression of Tom. "Real reassuring. I feel so safe."

Tom smiled and replied, "I mean no. No, there are any out here."

"Now you're mocking me," Megan huffed.

"I am not."

"Yes, you are."

Tom rolled over to once again face Megan. "I promise. I'm not."

"Then tell me."

"Ugh," Tom groaned. "I have no idea. I'm sure there are tons of coyotes around here…"

"Tons!" Megan exploded.

"Yeah, tons. But I have no idea if there are any without fur around here."

"I guess it doesn't matter what kills me when I go outside to squat piss in the middle of the night," Megan sarcastically exclaimed. "Could be a freakin' chupacabra or a coyote or a jaguar…" "Jaguar?" Tom exclaimed in disbelief.

"Yeah, jaguar. You said earlier they used to be here or could be here…"

"There are no jaguars here," Tom assured his girlfriend.

"You don't know what's out here waiting to kill us!" Megan stated. "You have no idea!"

15.

Hunter led Taylor outside the main building and into the darkness. Hunter lit a cigarette and offered one to Taylor who nodded silently in acceptance. Taylor lit his offered Marlboro and stared out upon the desolate ranchland illuminated by stars and a half moon before him.

"You believe him?" Hunter asked, breaking the silence. "Because I kind of do."

"You believe your men were killed by albino baboons?" Taylor answered with a question, unsure if Hunter was being serious or not.

"I don't know," Hunter admitted. "I don't know if it was baboons. Probably wasn't. But I do think what ripped his crew apart was animal. Not human."

"What kind of animal lives down there, deep underground in a sealed cave?" Taylor scoffed.

"Might not have been sealed," Hunter theorized. "Julio said they couldn't see the other side. Doesn't mean there's not one or that there's a tunnel that leads up and out."

Taylor killed his cigarette and snuffed the butt into the sandy earth with his boot.

He listened as Hunter explained that the area of the border the goat ranch sat upon had gone through dramatic changes in the past few years. Deep irrigation canals had been dug outward from the Rio Grande. Quarries had been torn into mountain bases and hills were leveled for earth and gravel. On the American side, construction crews had been pounding steel beams up to 20 feet into the earth in order to construct a border wall. The area has seen fracking by big oil companies, and as a result, earthquakes had occurred and sinkholes appeared. Hunter theorized that one of these activities had opened the cave system Julio and his men tapped into. Animals had traveled downward and become lost in the darkness. They were starving and once fresh meat came upon them, they attacked with fervor.

"What kind of animals are you thinking?" Taylor queried.

"Cougar. Bear. Coyote maybe. Who knows? But whatever ripped apart Julio's brother was big enough and strong enough to knock his fat ass down and had claws and teeth sharp enough leave him looking like he'd been run through a meat grinder."

Hunter's words sent Taylor's memory back to Afghanistan to a time he and his unit were investigating a cave system in the mountains of the Tora Bora. The cave opening was natural. The tunnel system it led to was not. Taylor and his men had winded their way through 300 meters of abandoned, carved-out terrorist highway when they encountered an Asiatic black bear denned up among the remains of an empty food cache. The animal looked sickly and partially emaciated yet lunged at him and his men with the ferocity of a wild beast. Taylor had put two shots into the bear and it still rushed forward at him as if it had been bit by horseflies. A final shot to the head put the bear down and sent the whole team into fits of hysterical laughter and joking about their Taliban hunt being turned into a bear hunt.

A similar situation could have befallen Julio and his team of diggers. And given that none of them were trained soldiers, armed and ready, it could explain the heavy loss of life. Taylor exited his thoughts to agree with Hunter's theory that it could have been an animal that took out the tunnel workers then added that whatever was down there would be found and killed soon enough.

Hunter agreed and offered, "Come on. Let's go meet the team. And have some fun."

16.

The old bunkhouse smelled of beer and cigar smoke, tequila, and cigarettes. Despite these remnants of vice, the interior of the building appeared to be a place of health and preparedness. The room contained weights and exercise equipment, gym mats, and two heavy bags hanging from the ceiling. Footlockers and hard cases of weaponry and military gear were stacked against the wall and at the end of every bed.

The group of six men and women stood and cheered in mock revelry at Hunter's return, quickly thrusting a cold beer in his and Taylor's hand. Hunter cracked a few jokes about his absences and how he'd found Taylor living under a highway overpass with a sign asking for work then introduced him to the team. They were:

Mitch Pearce, a former G4S Secure Solutions Agent in his late 30s. He stood 6'2", sported a five-inch-long bushy, black beard, and proudly wrapped his linebacker build in a skin-tight T-shirt that was cut to reveal his biceps the size of small hams. His khaki cargo shorts were baggy and frayed and looked like they had occasionally been used to clean the filth from the bottom of his long-worn flip-flops.

Tom Nickerson, a 5'10", slim-built former DEA Agent from Arizona who, after realizing the folly and stupidity of the U.S. War on Drugs, joined the cartel to make money.

Sergio Agüera, a 5'9" Mexican National with the build of a professional soccer player, spent the last year working every hellhole Academi sent him to before coming home to join the Acuña Cartel.

Kerri Ruck, 5'3" of self-proclaimed, "100% Texas born and raised bull dyke that'll rip you a new one and then some if you call me that and ain't my friend."

Marquis Jordan, an African-American from the mean streets of Chicago, who even at 40 years old still sent half his paycheck home to his "momma" while referring to her as his number one gal.

And Louise "Lou" Drake, who was 5'9" of steel-cut muscle poured into a feminine form of curves and dirty-blonde hair.

Taylor finished his beer, took a fresh one offered from Ruck then a cigar from Hunter, and listened to the team joke and share stories of times afield and of doing the cartel's bidding. Everyone promised that the work was far and few between but the pay and benefits beyond compare. Taylor laughed and said that he was shocked a Mexican drug cartel had a Human Resources Officer and even more so at his explained his benefits. The team admitted that they too were shocked but that the cartel had lived up to each and every promise they made toward the team.

"I just hope taxidermy's part of my benefits package," Pearce said. "'Cause if I take out some cave monkeys tomorrow, you know I'm gonna get one mounted!"

The team laughed and Ruck added to the fun by saying that a monkey was about the only thing Pearce ever could mount. Pearce raised his beer in salute at the insult then accepted a huge bear hug from Ruck and laughed some more. The drinking and the camaraderie grew late into the evening and by the time they all retired, Taylor felt that he had made the right decision in finally accepting Hunter's job offer.

17.

Dejah Lopez did her best to keep up with her mother and uncle, but they and the group they were a part of were moving too fast, weaving through the terribly difficult thorn scrub brush on narrow goat trails with only the moon and stars to light the way. Keeping up was made even more difficult given Dejah's ill-fitting shoes. The sneakers had passed down through three older sisters before they got to Dejah and they consisted of nothing but paper-thin leather and slick rubber soles.

Dejah's mother hurried her along once more with a quick snap of her wrist and Dejah felt her shoulder pull. She released a small cry of discomfort and was quickly shushed by her mother and those ahead of her. Dejah pouted at the instructions and grimaced but followed her mother through the tangles of mesquite and huisache trees to a small opening littered with plastic bags and water bottles, discarded clothing, and other sundries.

"We cross just over there," the leader of the group whispered. "The water is only about two feet deep but the current's pretty strong so stay alert."

The group nodded and some took on looks of worry or concern.

"Crossing the river is when we're out in the open and the most vulnerable so remember to hurry and keep as quiet as you can," the leader continued.

Again, the group nodded.

The travelers tightened up their backpacks and cinched their belts and made sure their bags were tied tight over their shoulders. Some wore looks of excitement, others worry, and others crossed themselves and said prayers. Dejah's mom crossed herself and asked God for protection and for him to lead her and Dejah to their family that was already established and waiting for them in Austin. Dejah listened to her mother's prayers and crossed herself as well then tried one more time to tie her shoes so that they would be tight on her feet.

The frontrunner led the group of travelers out of the clearing and down a narrow path that wove through the scrub and onto the bank of the Rio Grande. The shore was muddy with a sprinkling of rocks and gravel that glowed in the moonlight. The group followed in a single-file line as they were led down the bank and into the river. Dejah held her mother's hand tight but then broke free of her grip when her shoe became submerged in the mud at the river's edge. Dejah leaned down and pulled the ratty sneaker back on her feet.

"Hurry, *mija*," Dejah's mother scolded in a deep whisper. She grabbed Dejah's hand once more and led her into the river with a firm jerk.

The water was warm but considerably cooler than the air, and Dejah's body shuddered as a shiver ran up her spine. She followed her mother the best she could but pushing through waist-high water—even while being pulled along—was difficult and the river was wider than she thought it would be. She was a third of the way across when her shoe slipped from her foot. She pulled her hand from her mother and leaned into the black water to grab it before it slid completely off. The current grabbed Dejah and pulled her forward and under. She spun over and came to the surface to breathe and to right herself, but the pull of the water wouldn't allow her to plant her feet. She struggled to stand or to turn around, but the water became deeper and faster. She saw her mother and another from the group reaching out across the darkness, as if willing her to stop or to return. She tried to call to them but instead swallowed a mouthful of silt-heavy water.

The current threw her against a rock and the sudden pain in her back brought tears to boil in her eyes. She spun around and tried to grab the rock that had momentarily paused her race down the shallow water but wasn't able to and slipped by it. She turned in the current over and over and fought to stand or at least to right herself so that she might swim. The current slammed Dejah into another rock and then another. She grabbed ahold of the next one and pulled herself up and partially out of the water. She thrust her legs underneath her and finally found the river bottom. She stood to realize that the water was now only to her upper thigh. She brushed her long black hair off her face, caught her breath, then studied her surroundings.

The moon and stars cast light down on a bank of large rocks and boulders. The treeline was high above a jumble of car-sized rocks. She looked for her mother and the group upstream but saw that the river curved and that she had been swept down and around at least one bend. She coughed, wadded toward the shore, and climbed out of the river. Both her shoes were gone, and she was suddenly cold.

"Don't yell," she told herself in a heavy whisper. "The man said not to make noise."

She ambled gingerly up the steep bank on bare feet and away from the river. She serpentined through and over rocks, broken limbs, and damp vegetation. Dejah made it twenty yards from the river when the vegetation between two rocks she stepped upon gave way, and she plummeted downward and into a deep hole. She landed hard on her leg, and her ankle gave and twisted. Dejah looked up at the hole she fell through some twenty feet above her, rubbed her ankle, and wept.

18.

Héctor Abrego collected his thoughts as the rest of the travelers did their best to console a hysterical Maria. From what Hector could tell, Dejah had lost her footing and was swept downstream by the swift current. Through convulsions of pain and sorrow, Maria explained that Dejah was a good swimmer and was absolutely, without a doubt, alive. Not only that, but Dejah was probably waiting for the group just a little bit downstream.

Héctor listened to the mother's pleas then laid out the realities of the situation.

"If we don't make the truck at the scheduled time, they'll leave," Hector assured the group. "And the nearest place to hitch your ride is another 15 miles in."

"I'm not going back," one traveler blurted out.

"Neither am I," another added.

"We have to find her," Maria wept. "We have to."

The group talked to among themselves and agreed to spend a half hour looking for the child before returning to the trail and ultimately making their way to the truck.

"After a half hour, I'm taking everybody to the truck," Héctor decreed before looking to Maria and adding, "Everybody that's wanting to go."

Maria was hysterical at the decision of the group and began to argue and make threats. She was consoled by her brother Carlos who said that a half hour was all the time they needed to find Dejah.

Héctor led the caravan down the muddy banks of the river on the American side. He kept the group close to the treeline and in the shadows. They had traveled only 10 minutes downstream before Héctor spotted a dark figure kneeling at the side of the river some 50 yards away.

"Dejah!" Maria called out into the darkness.

Many in the group responded to Maria's call with immediate directives to shush and to be quiet.

Maria nodded and with Carlos's hand in hers, ran toward the still-kneeling figure.

"Dejah, *mija. Mija!*" Maria called in a loud whisper as she ran forward. "Dejah!"

The figure turned and rose from its crouched position and growled. The night sky reflected a maw of ivory fangs chattering in some primordial cry of excitement. Maria's brain registered the danger of the situation, and she and her brother both skidded to a halt. The creature's jaws opened to release a scream of warning and attack. Teeth flashed and vaulted through the air and toward her.

Maria didn't feel her neck slice open.

Only the flood of warmth that poured from it and the sudden euphoria release it brought about.

19.

Dejah stifled her tears at the sound. It was the faintest of calls, the whisper of her name on the wind. She stood then grimaced at the pain from her ankle and stared up at the moonlit hole high above her in hope. The call came once more, this time louder and more distinct.

"Dejah, *mija. Mija*!" it called.

Dejah called in return.

She screamed for her mother as loud as she could.

Then stopped.

In between her cries for her mother, she heard something.

She heard the growl of an angry dog.

The screams of men.

The howling of what must have been a pack of wild dogs, their cries angry and feral.

She heard the crying of women.

And the angry yells of men.

The hole above her suddenly eclipsed.

Dejah stared upward and made out the shape of a man's upper body crawling into the narrow opening.

"Down here! I'm down here!" she cried.

The man above her was jerked backward and out of the opening. He cried and his cries were answered by a guttural roar.

The wet sounds of feeding.

Of bones snapping.

Several objects rained down from the opening.

They hit the cave floor with a series of light thuds.

Dejah bent down to identify the objects.

They were severed fingers.

Severed human fingers.

Dejah collapsed to the ground, weeping in fear, and scooted away from the light and into the darkness.

20.

Taylor's dreams were fueled by alcohol, nicotine, fatigue, and the anticipation of what was to come. He's mind took him through vivid memories of death and loss, serving and killing, compassion and regret.

He saw his daughter at her happiest.

Her prettiest.

He watched her celebrate birthdays and Christmases, long summer days at the lake and winter days accompanying her father afield for deer hunts. He watched again the courtship of his wife and their wedding, their making love, and their welcoming their daughter.

The joys of life gave way to the harsh realities of a soldier.

Taylor watched himself cross deserts of burning sand, trudge through tunnels of stone and rock, and walk through villages of the oppressed and the starving. He saw himself fight for his team and for his life. He lay witness to his protecting life and taking life.

These images twisted and warped and transported him to his daughter's hospital room. He stood over his baby girl, once so innocent and pure, now a lifeless shell connected to machine after machine via tubes and needles. He saw her gravestone. Watched his wife screaming blame after blame and insult after insult at him. He saw the .45 he held under his chin and the tears in his eyes that for some reason kept him from pulling the trigger.

He awoke and scanned the room that was his reality. He let his eyes adjust to the dark then pulled on a pair of pants and unlaced boots. He made his way past others of his team that slept on beds or against the wall and stepped outside.

Hunter stood on the porch, smoking a cigarette. He acknowledged Taylor with a nod and the offer of a cigarette and his lighter. Taylor took them both and gave a nod of thanks. He lit a cigarette and handed the lighter back to Hunter. The two men stood in the dark, smoking in silence, in an understanding that need not be spoken.

21.

Cletus Lee King didn't hate the border wall.

He loved the idea.

Loved that his country would be illegal free after its completion.

What Cletus Lee didn't like about the wall was that he had to supervise its construction.

This meant hour after hour of driving down half-assed roads carved from the brush to the middle of absolutely nowhere. The roads were pockmarked and driving over them, even in his Ford Super Duty F-350 at 20 miles per hour, shook his almost 300 pounds of morbidly obese body around like a plate full of Jell-O in the hands of someone in the midst of an epileptic seizure.

The rattling about his truck was so bad that Cletus Lee couldn't drink coffee or beer—depending on the time of day—as the liquid splashed all about the truck cab and all over his clothing. Not only that, but the crappy roads had caused him to miss his spit cup on numerous occasions, and more than once, he had exited his truck looking like a kid with a leaky diaper had been rolling around on his lap.

The road to Angel's camp was especially horrible and long. It was almost 20 miles in length, cut through some of the thickest stands of cedar and mesquite Cletus Lee had ever seen, going over and through hills, outcroppings of limestone, and other rock. There was no way to travel the road other than in four-wheel-drive and its proximity to a town of any significance was the reason Angel and his crew were camping on site. They'd apparently done well at their assigned duties as Cletus Lee hadn't heard nearly a peep from them.

Until yesterday.

Angel had called on his satellite phone with word that his boys had accidentally dug into a cavern that looked like it could swallow their equipment whole. Cletus Lee told Angel to sit tight until he could get out there to survey the situation, and Cletus Lane left his office at five AM that morning to do just that.

It took him almost four hours to make it to Angel's camp and when he did finally arrive, he was furious that no one rushed up to his truck to meet him. Cletus Lee angrily threw his truck in park and exited the vehicle. He stepped to the brush line to relieve himself and then walked back to the truck to retrieve his Copenhagen. He placed a huge wad in his lower lip and scanned the campsite before him.

He saw hammocks and chairs, empty bottles and cans, food wrappers and half-empty water bottles, and a sea of cigarette butts.

"Goddamn pigs, the lot of them," Cletus Lee exclaimed aloud before spitting a huge mixture of spittle and phlegm up on the ground. "Goddamn pigs!"

He walked from the truck and into the campsite. He walked past the garbage toward the Porta Potty. He knocked on the door and, when one no one answered, opened it to find it empty. He turned from the portable commode and caught the glare of the early morning sun reflecting off a mirror on the excavator parked somewhere past a stand of mesquite. He walked toward it.

The expanse before Cletus Lee exploded in darkness. Dozens of buzzards, each black as midnight and carrying a wingspan of upwards of five feet, vaulted from the ground, from low-lying limbs, and from cacti. They turned the sky dark with their forms and their wings stirred a cloud of stench, decay, and rot. The air thundered with their flapping wings and the screeches of scavengers surprised and avoiding danger. Cletus Lee clutched his chest in surprise and fought to catch his breath. He watched the vultures fly higher and higher then circle in wait for his absence.

Cletus Lee's eyes were brought back down to earth by the deafening buzzing of flies. He trained in on the source of the noise to see what was left of a human form twisted and mutilated in death and by the fight for scraps by animals and avian prey. He stumbled backward at the site and vomited. He wiped his mouth with the back of his hand and stepped closer to what he saw was the first of several half-eaten human forms. He knelt next to the first body and studied it for any sign of identification, but the almost complete lack of a face made that task impossible. He thought of checking the body for a wallet then thought the better of it. He started to stand than noticed a print forced into the blood-soaked mud that pooled outward from the body.

It looked like a child's handprint.

Only different.

The fingers were that of a child, but the palm was twice as long as it should have been. The pinky and thumb were oddly spaced and situated further away from the rest of the fingers. Cletus Lee wiped his mouth once more, returned to his truck, and retrieved a Taurus Judge handgun from the center consul. He nervously checked to make sure it was loaded then put it in the waistband of his pants at the small of his back. He put a fresh dip of Copenhagen in his sour mouth then dialed 911 on his satellite phone.

22.

Dejah awoke in the dark and in pain. At first, she didn't know where she was but soon remembered her ordeal and what had transpired that led her to where she was now.

She was in a cave of some sort, alone, hungry, and scared.

She had no idea where her mother was or what happened to the rest of the group. She remembered the man in the hole above her, his screams, and how his fingers rained down upon her. She shuddered this thought out of her mind and stood. She was relieved to find that her ankle didn't hurt nearly as bad as it had only last night. She was also relieved to see that she wasn't in total darkness. In addition to the manhole-sized beam of light shimmering through the hole she fell through, there were other beams of light. More like pinpoints of light, these narrow splinters shone down from cracks high above to reveal a huge cavern. It was a dark expanse that seemed to go on and on forever. It reminded Dejah of being out under a star-filled sky.

Her thoughts were interrupted by the faintest sound of rushing water. She stared out into the void and saw that one of the needles of light pointed downward to a small stream. She edged down the slippery rock bank and toward the water, feeling before her with outstretched arms for dangers in the dark. Each step took her deeper into the cave, and she shuffled her feet before her to ensure she didn't fall or trip on something unseen. She reached the stream and kneeled beside it. The light cast down on an area the size of her foot and in that she could see that the water was relatively clear and free of debris. She cupped her hands and drank. The water was warm but tasted fine. She drank four more handfuls then made her way back up the steep rock toward the hole that she'd fallen through. Without looking down, she kicked the fingers from within the light and into the darkness, feeling with her feet that the area was clear of dangers, to directly underneath the hole and shouted upward for her mother. Her cries echoed back at her and waved throughout the cave. She continued calling for her mother then changed her call to that of help.

A sudden shrill call from deep within the cave caught her off guard. She stared out into the darkness and toward its source but could see nothing other than a few narrow needles of light. The call echoed across the void once more. It sounded like the scream of some animals although she couldn't tell what kind. Despite its far away distance, Dejah suddenly became more scared. She lowered herself to the ground and sat holding her knees to her chest in fear, hoping that she wouldn't hear the cry again and that her mother would come get her soon.

23.

Jared climbed down the extension ladder to join Tom in the cave. The two men shone their flashlights out of the light from the opening above and into the darkness that spread outward in every direction.

"How far down is the actual floor?" Jared asked, shining his light down off the pile of bones, rock, and years of debris that he and Tom stood upon.

"Maybe 30 feet," Tom offered. "Animals have been falling down here for centuries. Maybe a millennium."

Jared wiped his brow and coughed.

"You gonna throw up again?" Tom asked, chuckling.

"Ha. Ha. Ha. No," Jared mocked. "It's just hot down here. I thought it would be cooler."

"I thought it be smaller," Tom admitted, still scanning the darkness with his light.

"And it stinks to high heaven down here," Jared exclaimed. "What is that? Is that shit? A whole lot of bat shit?"

"I don't think so," Tom speculated. "If there was a bat colony down here, we would've seen them fly out last night. Or fly back this morning."

"Something's been down here shitting," Jared replied.

"Rats maybe…"

"Monkey shit!" Jared suddenly exclaimed.

"What?" Tom asked, turning to face Jared.

"It's not bat shit. It's monkey shit. I knew it smelled familiar."

Tom stared at Jared in question.

"My roommate works in a lab where they've got a few monkeys. Smells just like that down here."

"You think there's monkeys down here? In a cave? In South Texas?"

"No, of course not. I'm just saying the smell down here reminds me of that. Reminds me of monkeys."

24.

"You've heard my jokes about it and my wise-ass comments over a few beers last night," Hunter began. "But here's the official detail of what our mission is."

"A few beers?" Pearce scoffed. "I shared at least 10 with you myself."

Hunter shot Pearce a dirty look and a half smile then proceeded.

"As I was saying. Twelve of our 13 tunnelers broke into an unexpected cavern or cave. They were attacked by something and all, but Julio was killed."

Hunter paused to allow everyone in the room to give Julio a look then continued. "Julio is the only witness and he tells us, quite convincingly, that he was attacked by baboons."

Some in the room scoffed while others rolled their eyes.

"Our boss, Mr. Alvarado, theorizes that what actually happened was that a rival group tunneled in on our boys and took them out."

"Is it possible?" Nickerson asked. "That mercs could be confused for monkeys or whatever?"

Hunter stood at the front of the room and thought for a moment before answering. "I don't know. I honestly don't know. Could've been some guys down there in light color camo or body armor…"

"I know what I to see," Julio interrupted from the side of the room.

All the room looked to Julio. He still wore a face of loss and trauma but also of sincerity.

"I know what I to see," Julio replied. "I know."

"I don't care who it was or what it was," Hunter began anew. "Whatever it is, we're going to eliminate the problem ASAP so we can get some boys back down there to digging.

"I'm glad to hear you say that."

All eyes in the room darted to the door where Miguel now stood. His business attire dress was in sharp contrast to the tactical wear that dominated the room. "Because we are losing a great deal of money by the tunnel not being completed."

Miguel paused and entered the room. He stood next to Hunter then looked to him for approval. Hunter gestured *be my guest* with his hand and Miguel began again once more.

"This tunnel is a sizable investment but one that will earn 400 to 500 times its cost once the first shipment of fentanyl makes it across.

Each day that I don't have a truck driving through it represents a loss of tens of millions of dollars."

Julio paused once more to allow the numbers and the severity of opening the tunnel to register with the people in the room. He then turned to Hunter and apologized, "I didn't mean to interrupt…to hijack your meeting with a financial report."

"No problem," Hunter insisted. "You're always welcome."

"I actually came in to hear Captain Taylor's ideas," Miguel continued. "Based on his experiences in Afghanistan, I'm sure whatever he has planned will be quite interesting."

Miguel stepped back into the doorway and watched as Taylor stood. Hunter dimmed the lights and Taylor took his place before a hand-drawn map that was projected on the screen at the front of the room.

"The tunnel begins here in the barn and is currently closed off via a hastily reinforced garage door. The interior of the tunnel measures almost seven feet tall and six and a half feet wide which is barely enough room to drive a modified truck through. A single line of lights runs along the ceiling with a bulb every few feet. The walls and floor are packed earth or rock."

Taylor paused then, seeing that he still had everyone's attention and understanding, continued.

"Julio and his men made it almost a mile and a half before breaking into a larger opening and being attacked. We have no idea how large this opening is, if it was man-made, or what, if anything, in the way of aggressors are within it." Taylor paused again then stepped away from the screen. He looked upon the team and addressed them on a more personal level.

"I know the measurements I gave you seem tight, but I assure you they are not. Most of the tunnels I dredged through in Stan Land were a third of that size. I have no idea what attacked Julio and his men, but I do know that it used surprise and the dark to its advantage."

Most in the makeshift station room nodded in agreement.

"And we'll do the same. Each one of you, including Julio, will be outfitted with either night vision or thermal imagery goggles."

Taylor saw puzzlement wash over Miguel and Julio's faces.

"Basically, thermal imaging sees heat," Taylor explained.

Miguel nodded in understanding.

Julio still looked confused.

Taylor disregarded the latter and returned to his team.

"We'll go in two-by-two with me and Hunter in the lead and Agüera and Ruck pulling up the rear."

Agüera and Ruck nodded in agreement. Agüera held his hand to Ruck for a fist bump that was denied with a smirk and a dismissive wave of the hand. The room exploded into laughter and howls of how Agüera was *dissed*.

"Only problem I expect we'll have his line of sight," Taylor continued. "Given the heavy slope of the tunnel, we won't have visual very far ahead of us regardless of what goggles we're wearing. So slow and steady is the name of the game. If or when we encounter hostiles, command will revert back to Hunter. Any questions?"

"Where will Julio be?" Nickerson asked.

"He'll be behind me," Taylor replied. "He knows the tunnel. I need him up front with me."

Nickerson nodded, as did a few others in the room.

Miguel did not nod in agreement.

He didn't believe Julio and found his story ridiculous, a complete waste of time. He was only allowing Julio to live as he was the only tunneler left and so the only one who could guide the team to where the ambush took place. Miguel told Hunter that he expected Julio to be dealt with accordingly once his story about killer apes was proven to be a complete fabrication.

Taylor brought Miguel's train of thought to a standstill. "Any other questions?" he continued.

Miguel stepped front and center once more. "Not a question, Captain, but a promise to you and your team. You all open the tunnel by this time tomorrow and you are each looking at a $10,000 bonus."

The team exploded into cheers and calls of excitement.

Hunter clapped his hands together and shouted over the noise, "Let's saddle up and earn that bonus."

26.

Border Patrol Agents Joel Andrews and Champe Carter exited their Chevy Suburban and made their way toward Cletus Lee who stood panting in the early morning heat next to his pickup.

"Are you Mr. Kane?" Agent Andrews asked nervously, palming the firearm in his side holster.

"King. Not Kane," Cletus Lee angrily explained. "I'm Cletus Lee. I called this mess in to you boys."

"And, are you an American citizen, Mr. King?" Agent Carter asked with pen and pad in his hand.

"Hell, yes I'm American. I'm a White, God-fearing, Christian Republican. And my name is Cletus Lee King. It don't get much more American than that."

"And are you armed, sir?" Agent Andrews asked. "Because you seem rather agitated and for our own safety…."

Cletus Lee raised his hands and spit a few ounces of tobacco spittle upon the ground. "I got a pistol in my back waistband. I've got a concealed carry card in my wallet. And I'm not agitated."

"That's just what an agitated individual would say," Agent Andrews explained.

Agent Carter placed his notepad into his front shirt pocket, made his way to behind Cletus Lee, and pulled the pistol from his waistband.

"We'll return this to you once you calm down," Agent Andrews explained.

"That ain't going to happen any time real soon, I tell ya," Cletus Lee said, dropping his hands. "I'm starting to regret calling you boys. Y'all ask about my citizenship, take my gun—"

"You called about some dead illegals," Agent Carter interrupted.

"No," Cletus Lee corrected. "I called you boys about my construction crew back there being dead. I mean, sure, some of them are illegals, but most ain't. Half of 'em ain't."

"Did you know it's against the law to knowingly employ illegal workers?" Agent Carter inquired.

Cletus Lee exploded in laughter then mocked, "No? Really? I had no idea."

"Yes, really," Agent Carter assured him. "A person commits a federal felony when he or she—"

"Whatever. This is Texas. I'll hire who I want," Cletus Lee barked. "Y'all wanna see what I found or not. I mean, y'all come out here to look at murdered folks and instead all y'all are doing is—"

"We don't know that anyone has been murdered," Agent Andrews interrupted.

"Oh yeah, the boys back there committed suicide by eating themselves down to the bone overnight."

Agent Andrews and Agent Carter looked to one another then to Cletus Lee then back to one another.

"Please lead us to the bodies," Agent Andrews requested.

Cletus Lee did as he was asked and, as it had before, the sky turned black with the sudden explosive flight of buzzards. Agents Andrew and Carter gagged at the onslaught smell of rot and decay that overwhelmed the area and swatted at the clouds of buzzing flies that nearly engulfed them.

"Is this one of the individuals you called the agency about?" Agent Andrews asked, trying not to vomit.

Cletus Lee turned in disgust, rolled his eyes, and said to himself, "A couple of goddamn rocket scientists I got out here."

"I'm sorry, sir. I didn't hear you," Agent Andrews admitted.

Cletus Lee turned around to address the agents.

"Yes, sir," he condescendingly began again. "That there dead mutilated body is one of the dead mutilated bodies I called y'all about. Them other dead mutilated bodies back there too."

Agent Andrews and Agent Carter nodded to one another then knelt next to the remains of the first body. They looked the body up and down, nodded to one another, and rose.

"Chainsaw," Agent Andrews and Agent Carter said in unison. "Chainsaw."

"Chainsaw?" Cletus Lee guffawed. "Chainsaw what?"

"It is our assessment that this individual and I'm guessing the others, if they look like this poor gentleman, were killed by chainsaw-wielding cartel members," Agent Andrews decreed.

"Are you shitting me?" Cletus Lee exploded. "Chainsaws don't eat folks to the bone, 'n' they don't leave bite marks."

"Buzzards," Agent Carter replied. "Buzzards ate these individuals. You saw them fly away."

"Buzzards! They couldn't kill these folks and eat them down as far as they did in less than a day."

"It was a chainsaw that killed these men," Agent Andrews reiterated. "Buzzards are what ate them."

"What about this crazy footprint here?" Cletus Lee inquired, pointing at the odd-shaped cast in the bloody mud next to his boot.

"It appears to be that of a child," Agent Carter theorized.

"That's not a child print!" Cletus Lee's blood pressure was at the tipping point. He didn't know how much longer he could stand these two idiots. "Look at it. It's all deformed."

"Yes," Agent Andrews agreed. "It appears to be the footprint of a deformed child."

"A lot of deformed individuals try to enter America," Agent Carter explained. "After all, we have the best health care system in the world."

"And we are a very inclusive society," Agent Andrews added. "Americans don't bully the handicapped anymore."

Cletus Lee spit in utter disgust and declared, "Boys, there's something weird going on out here, and it ain't a Mexican drug cartel out for a day of chainsaw chop suey! If y'all don't pull your heads out, I'm afraid whatever's happened out here is going to bite you and yours in the ass big time."

27.

Despite the fact that they followed his command and that they followed military structures and procedures, Hunter's team wasn't military.

They were mercenaries.

And as such, Hunter let them choose their own weapons and what equipment they took into the field. Yes, today they'd all be issued night vision and thermal imaging goggles and radios, but everything else they took into the tunnel was of their own selection.

Hunter himself was wearing his standard outfit of a 5.11 tactical pants and shirt, custom boots, and body armor. He carried a Glock 19 pistol, an FN MK 16 CQC rifle, extra ammunition for both, a knife, flashlight, and a multi-tool. He also carried a small pack with a three-liter Camelback filled with water, several energy bars, and a first-aid kit.

Taylor's gear was similar. He wore the same style clothing as Hunter and the same thermal imaging goggles and body armor. He carried a Sig Sauer P320 chambered in 9mm, a LaRue Tactical Costa Edition AR-15 rifle, extra ammunition, a knife, two M84 percussion grenades, and a pack filled with water, energy bars, and extra batteries.

Pearce's massive build and thick black beard gave him the appearance of a barbarian from a fantasy film. The 18-inch socket machete he carried in addition to his Colt M4A1 SOPMOD rifle and Glock pistol made him appear even more so.

Nickerson wore worn fatigues from his DEA days and carried the same .40 Glock 22 pistol that he used during his career in the agency. He also carried a Heckler & Koch MP5A3 rifle and Ka-Bar knife.

Although not one for theatrics or flashiness, Agüera carried twin 1911 pistol's sporting ivory handles with silver and bejeweled Mexican eagle engraves. Agüera had taken his "pair of trophies" off a *sicario* from the Sinaloa Cartel sent to collect a bounty on his head. The hit man didn't succeed and Agüera picked up two new .45s as keepsakes. In addition, Agüera also carried an M4A1 Carbine rifle, Bench Made SOCP dagger, an ARDEC stun grenade, and several packs of Marlboros.

Like Agüera, Ruck also carried a sidearm she'd taken off someone with nefarious intentions. She had just turned 13 when she made the adult decision that her mother's live-in boyfriend would never hurt her or her mother again. Ruck waited for the right opportunity and found it on the night the man whose-name-she-refused-to say pulled a Beretta 9mm on her mom in yet another one of his booze and drug-fueled tirades. Ruck put a frying pan to his head from behind then watched in pure bliss as he hit the floor and stayed there bleeding out for 20 minutes. When the man came to, Ruck was holding his pistol to his head. Ruck said she'd love to pull the trigger but had a social studies project she'd worked really hard on due the next day and hated to miss turning it in because of all the police drama that would surely come from her putting a bullet through his, "worthless piece of shit head." Mom's now ex-boyfriend agreed that shooting him would definitely mean Ruck would miss school the next day and promised to leave immediately. Ruck held a pistol on him all the way to his truck.

Ruck worried that he might return but that fear was erased when the police came to inform her and her mother that he'd died in a car wreck shortly after leaving their trailer house. The bash to his head delivered by Ruck and his subsequent loss of blood combined with all the alcohol and narcotics in his system caused him to fall asleep at the wheel and run off a highway overpass.

Ruck also carried a Daniel Defense M4A1 rifle and knife.

Jordan outfitted himself with the same make of clothing and firearms that he used during his two combat tours in Afghanistan. Not because he was too lazy to research anything different, but because they'd served him well. He saw no reason to change what worked and the low-cost of surplus military gear fit his thrifty nature well. For weapons, Jordan carried a Heckler & Koch MP5A3 rifle and Sig Sauer P320 chambered in .45 ACP.

Drake carried a Radical Firearm AR-15 rifle, Glock 19 pistol, pry bar, and a little something extra she recently picked up online.

"What the hell is that?" Hunter asked as his team assembled outside the wooden barricade that blocked the tunnel's entrance.

"Flamethrower," Drake replied with serious pride.

"Flamethrower?" Hunter both exclaimed and asked in disbelief.

"That it is," Drake replied. "One all American flamethrower made and sold by America's favorite inventor Elon Musk."

"The car guy?" Hunter asked.

"The one and only," Drake answered

"His cars come with flamethrowers now?" Hunter seriously inquired.

"Don't know," Drake answered. "I just bought one of his flamethrowers. I'm not into electric cars. I'm more of a diesel kind of gal."

"Time's wasting," Taylor interrupted. "Sun's going down. I want to be at the massacre point when it's dark above and below the earth."

"It's your mission," Hunter assured Taylor with a smile.

Taylor stood before the plywood and timber reinforced garage door. He held his rifle supported by a Spec-Ops Patrol Sling before him and at the ready. He turned his head away from the group and whispered into his radio, "COMMS check."

The team answered with their names one by one and Taylor turned to face them.

"We're going underground and into a pitch-black void," Taylor commanded. "Do not let your mind get the best of you. Trust the gear, stay tight, and stay focused."

The team nodded and gave thumbs up and formed two lines before the sealed tunnel. Taylor pointed to Juan and Arturo and they quickly took their places at the barricade. Taylor turned and pointed to José who stood next to a bank of light switches at the far wall. José nodded, flipped the switch, and the windowless interior of the barn was plunged into total darkness.

28.

Dejah felt like she was in a fevered dream.

Her state reminded her of the time she had the flu. She had laid in bed for three days, unsure if she was awake or not. Things would happen and she'd later wonder if they had truly occurred.

Had her mother really bathed her in bed?

Had her grandmother really brought her soup?

These encounters had seemed real, but Dejah couldn't be sure when recalling them.

The same held true of her time in the cave.

The view through the hole above her showed dusk.

Had she really been alone in the cave she'd fallen into for almost a full day?

Or had it been two days?

She remembered taking a nap in the beam of light that shone through the point of her entrance earlier in the day. Had she slept through the day then the night and into another day?

She couldn't be sure.

She stared at the sky high, high above her and wondered.

Wondered when her mother would finally come get her and what they'd eat to celebrate their being back together again. She really hoped that the reunion would happen soon, as she was starving.

After all, she hadn't eaten anything in a day.

Or was it two days?

She remembered trying to quell her hunger with several trips to the small stream that flowed beneath the pinpoint of light deeper within the cave. Her drinking did little to ease her hunger and the light—all the lights—were now gone.

Did the lack of light mean the dogs or whatever they were would start growling again?

She'd heard them lots of times during her time in the cave. Sometimes they'd bark; other times they'd shriek or howl. They sounded like dogs, kind of like dogs but she couldn't be sure.

Not because she couldn't remember but because their cries were so faint and came from so far away.

They were still scary though. The sounds they made didn't sound like they were friendly dogs.

Not at all.

They sounded mean and angry.

Dejah hoped maybe with the coming of night they'd go to sleep.

29.

Taylor dropped his thermal imaging goggles from his helmet and onto his face. The lightless void before him came into stereovision and he watched as the blaze-white heat signatures of Juan and Arturo opened the barricaded garage door. Taylor nodded and the team entered the tunnel slowly and deliberately. They had walked maybe 10 yards when the team dropped into the kneeling position. Taylor turned and watched as Juan and Arturo shut the doors behind them.

The team paused for a time to see if the noise of the door attracted any attention from deeper inside the tunnel. When none came, the team moved forward with Taylor's line hugging the left-hand side of the tunnel and Hunter's line taking the right side. The floor they hiked upon was mostly loose dirt and made for easy and silent movement. They'd gone another 10 minutes in when Taylor brought the group to a halt and knelt next to wallow in the earth. He pulled Julio closer and whispered, "What happened here?" The group listened on the COMM channel as Julio sniffed and breathed into his microphone, trying to hold back tears.

"I almost to give up," Julio whispered. "I could no drag no more. I fall. Try to stand again."

Taylor put his hand on Julio's back in a sign of compassion. He held it there for a moment then stood and took his team further and deeper into the tunnel.

The further they went into the Earth, the more stagnant the air became. The team's boots inadvertently kicked up sand and clouds of dust plumed from the floor. The team hugged the walls, occasionally and inadvertently an individual catching the wall with their shoulder or arm. Julio did this twice and each time recoiled in horror and away from the unseen that had reached from the darkness to grab him. This, along with the smell of the tunnel and seeing the spot where he had almost given up on dragging his brother's body back from hell, brought back a flood of emotions.

He felt the fear of that day.

The weakness of being able to crawl out from under his brother to help ward off the nightmares.

The rage of his brother's killing.

And the desperation to get his brother's body to safety.

Julio was brought out of his memories by Taylor's sudden stop. Julio almost ran into the heat signature before him and he shuffled his feet to keep from doing so. The team came to a halt and watched in either night or thermal vision as Taylor pointed to a spot on the tunnel ceiling some 15 yards before them. The heat signature was small, oval-shaped, and not much larger than a fist.

"Julio?" Taylor whispered.

"No bats when I here," Julio answered.

Taylor immediately analyzed the situation.

He theorized that the animal had entered the tunnel from a natural cave rather than a rival's newly dug tunnel. It took bats weeks if not months to accept a new roosting spot and them doing so while the area was under construction was most unlikely. *Still*, Taylor thought, *it doesn't mean soldiers couldn't have come through a natural cave. All they would need was a way in.*

Taylor kept his thoughts to himself and led the team onward. They passed under the bat and it remained wedged in a small crack on the tunnel ceiling, unfazed or unaware by the team passing beneath it.

The team traveled onward, each step taking them further and deeper under the earth. The temperature dropped and the air grew more stale. They had hiked another 30 minutes without incident or sign of life of any kind when a draft was felt. The air was cooler, more humid, and carried with it the overwhelming stench of rot and decay, viscera and blood.

Julio panicked at the wretch. His mind flooded with the still-fresh memories of the attack. He couldn't breathe and the helmet and goggles the team was making him wear were too constrictive. He gasped for air but each and every breath filled his lungs with the taste of death. Taylor sensed Julio's change and brought the team to a halt. He turned to Julio and whispered, "You're fine. Take a deep breath. Relax."

Julio nodded in the darkness.

"We're not gonna let anything happen to you," Taylor continued. "Take a moment."

Julio nodded once more.

"Remember your deal with Colonel Hunter," Taylor added. "You'll be in America soon. You and your family."

The promise of a new life for him and his family washed over Julio. His mind left the tunnel and the pain of the attack and carried him to a better place, to land of unlimited possibilities. His breathing returned to normal and he felt confident in his being.

Taylor led the team forward. The stench grew worse and the air became even heavier. They moved forward silently and at the ready for anything and everything. Twenty minutes passed before they came upon the first signs of slaughter. One of the tunnelers lay splayed upon the tunnel floor. His body was free from clothing and his arms legs and torso free of meat. His intestines were twisted and coiled about him as if pulled from him and thrown aside by someone or something in a fit of rage.

Taylor and his team barely acknowledged the body and instead moved forward through the crack in the earth. They passed three more bodies, each mutilated beyond recognition and instead resembling caricatures of human forms as if fashioned from a fevered dream or by evil itself. The tunnel floor was littered with dried blood, viscera, and torn earth that told of struggle and carnage.

The team ventured another five yards and came to a site of ghastly proportions. Scattered among the digging equipment, propane tanks, and jumbled rock were the remains of six bodies, each partially dismembered in some form or fashion with some missing limbs, and others having faces shredded or left hanging from exposed bone. The air was putrid and made poisonous with the smell of offal and putrescence. The team snaked through the downed equipment and ravaged corpses to the door-sized entrance to the cave. They entered the cave one by one and each took in the vastness of the spectacle before them in their own way. Taylor ignored the wonder of the undiscovered and instead scanned it for fluctuations in temperature that would denote life. The cave was enormous but void of anything warm-blooded.

"Goggles up," Taylor commanded before switching channels on his COMM. "José, we're at the cave. Hit the lights."

30.

The lights in the tunnel flamed to life and flooded out of the entrance to the cave and into the cavern. Taylor, Hunter, Drake, Nickerson, and Pearce each turned on their flashlights and scanned the cave.

"Welcome to Hell," Nickerson joked.

"Funny, I thought it'd be hotter," Pearce said, laughing.

"I thought it'd be lighter," Ruck added.

Nickerson and Pearce looked to Jordan for explanation.

"Ya know," Ruck began. "To better see the misery you're spending eternity in."

"This thing is huge," Hunter announced in disbelief. "Absolutely incredible."

"There's tunnels going off in every direction," Taylor declared, scanning the far wall with his flashlight beam.

Taylor's study was interrupted by the fevered announcement of Pearce. "We've got ourselves a monkey!"

Taylor and Hunter turned toward the tunnel to see Pearce and Drake standing over a dark form. The team assembled around Pearce and Drake's discovery, and they all gazed upon a creature that only Julio ever believed existed.

The animal resembled a baboon except for his eyes, which appeared three to four times larger than they should have been on an animal of its size. The eyes were coal black and void of pupils. Its fur was dirty white and course. The claws on each of its feet were elongated, razor sharp, and pale ivory in color.

Pearce grabbed the dead animal by the scruff of its neck held it aloft. He dangled the beast before him and declared, "Hundred pounds. Maybe 105. Solid little bastard." Pearce dropped the animal to the ground and Nickerson asked the group, "Anyone got a tape?"

Taylor ignored the question and instead knelt at the creature's side. He spread his hand wide and used it to measure the carcass.

"About 45…48 inches long," Taylor dictated. "Tail's another 35 and looks like it's maybe 30 inches at the shoulder."

Taylor moved to the animal's maw and spread it wide.

"Canines are over an inch," Taylor added.

"It's male," Ruck observed.

"You know what one of those looks like?" Nickerson joked.

"A dick? Yeah, I'm looking at one," Ruck countered Nickerson.

Taylor continued to study the body. He ran his hands over several puncture wounds then looked up at Julio. "Your brother got 'em good."

Julio nodded and spat on the animal's face.

"Resilient little shits," Ruck barked. "The thing got stabbed that many times yet still managed to get this far out from the tunnel."

Hunter held out his hand to Julio and said, "You're going to America, my friend. I'm a man of my word and apparently so are you."

Julio stood in shock from the wave of emotions that crashed over him. He felt loss and anger, joy, and hope. He shook Hunter's hand then enveloped him in a bear hug.

"That's nice 'n' all," Pearce said. "I mean, this is a real touching moment, but can somebody tell me what the hell this thing is? And what the hell is it doing down here?"

"It's obviously a primate of some kind," Drake answered. "And the way they attacked, going for the face and fingers is consistent with that. Chimpanzees disable rivals or prey in the same manner."

All eyes turned to Drake. She shrugged her shoulders at their questioning eyes and disbelief and explained, "I don't date. I watch Animal Planet. And Planet Earth on BBC. That one's really good. They don't sugarcoat animals at all."

The team chuckled at Drake's explanation.

"You know all that from watching TV, Miss Lonelyheart?" Hunter chided.

"That and an unfinished master's degree in biology," Drake explained.

"Anything else?" Taylor inquired.

"Yeah, I ran out of money while working on my masters, so I joined the Army."

"No. I was talking about this animal here," Taylor corrected.

Again, the team laughed.

"I'd just be guessing," Drake continued.

"Please do," Taylor replied.

"All right, I'd say his eyes are in indicative that it's a troglobite…"

"Troglo what?" Nickerson snipped.

"Troglobites. Cave-dwelling animals. Or at least it's an animal that spends most of his time in the dark," Drake offered. "If this thing—or its kind—does leave the underground, it's doing so only at night."

"Sounds about right," Taylor agreed.

"Its claws look like they're adapted to digging," Drake continued. "I'm guessing it's pretty good at climbing as well."

"And ripping tunnelers to shreds," Nickerson added.

"I'm guessing it's good at ripping anything to shreds," Pearce tacked on.

"Why has no one seen these things?" Ruck asked, turning the conversation back to Drake

"Again, they're probably a nocturnal species," Drake theorized. "And this area's extremely remote. Aside from a few ranchers and oil workers, the area is void of humans. My guess is that they're an isolated species. Or what's left of one."

Hunter thought on Drake's theory for a moment then asked, "Why would an isolated species, that's probably never seen humans, attack humans? I thought animals that had never seen a human have no fear of them."

"That's true," Drake offered. "A recent example that would be scientists that discovered a new species of tree squirrel in Papua New Guinea that had absolutely no fear of humans whatsoever."

"Then why did this species attack the tunnelers and eat them, for Christ's sake?" Hunter pondered.

"Because they've encountered humans before," Taylor declared. "And they like the taste."

31.

"I don't see how," Drake countered. "Like I said, there's hardly any people out here. For a couple hundred miles in each direction."

"That's true of the people we know of," Taylor explained. "But this area's full of lots of people that don't want to be known about."

"Illegals?" Hunter both asked and offered.

Taylor nodded. "Illegals have been crossing here for decades. Trade caravans for centuries before."

Drake looked at Taylor in bemusement.

"I finished my master's." Taylor smirked. "It's in Texas History."

Drake smiled and Taylor continued.

"Point is, this area's seen a steady stream of folks over the last forty, fifty years, and none of the ones that went missing would ever be reported."

"People-eating baboons? I don't buy it," Jordan admitted. "Monkeys don't even eat meat... I mean, do they?"

"Primates eat meat, including other primates," Drake explained. "Chimps regularly hunt and kill Columbus monkeys for food. Orangutans have been observed eating squirrels and rodents."

"Baboons?" Taylor questioned.

"Oh yeah," Drake enthusiastically replied. "Baboons hunt and eat birds. Rodents. Small mammals. Other monkeys. I saw a troop of baboons take down this farmer's sheep on a YouTube video once. It was freakin' epic."

"So, we just discovered a new species?" Nickerson asked in clarification.

"Agartha baboons," Drake announced.

"What?" Nickerson pondered.

"Agartha baboons," Drake repeated. "I'm naming them. They're baboons and this is Agartha. The legendary city at the Earth's core."

Nickerson pantomimed looking around then exclaimed, "I don't see a city."

"Enough with the science and mythology lessons," Hunter snapped before turning to Julio. "How many were there?"

Julio shook his head and partially shrugged his shoulders. "I don't..."

"Guess," Hunter demanded.

"Fifteen. Twenty," Julio offered. "Maybe more."

"We can kill that many no problem," Nickerson promised.

"Mission's still the same, people," Hunter declared. "We eliminate the threat so that the tunnel can be completed."

"It's night now," Pearce reminded Hunter. "Drake said those things are nocturnal. Won't they be up top hunting or something?"

"Most likely," Drake agreed. "But most primates follow a social structure of assigned duties. While some are out hunting—if that's what they're doing—then there are most likely others left behind to protect their territory, tend to the young, etc."

"A real nuclear family," Nickerson spat sarcastically.

"Ruck," Hunter directed. "You 'n' Agüera keep watch over the entrance to the cave."

Ruck and Agüera nodded in agreement at their assignment.

"Julio," Hunter decreed. "You'll stay with them here in the tunnel."

Julio was still ecstatic about being told he was going to the United States and his nod of agreement toward Hunter showed as much.

Hunter looked to Taylor then waved his hand at the enormity of the cavern just outside the entrance he stood before. "Any ideas?" he asked.

Taylor directed his flashlight beam out of the tunnel and across the cavern toward a multitude of holes on the far side of the cave.

"Some of those are tunnels," Taylor stated. "I say we follow the one that smells the worst."

"Yeah, this whole cave reeks of ammonia. Like a damn zoo exhibit," Nickerson complained.

"All the more reason to go off them smelly bastards," Jordan declared.

32.

Taylor and the remainder of his team lowered their goggles and ventured forward into the total darkness of the cavern. The cavern floor was mostly rock worn smooth by some ancient river long dried up, and the air was weighted with humidity and the heavy ammonia-laden smell of primate urine and feces. The main cavern was 200 to 250 yards across and ended at a wall honeycombed with tunnels. The team stood looking at the wall and the tunnels that ran into it. Some of them walked a few feet from the others in study while others looked to Taylor to see what he would do.

"This one," Taylor said walking forward toward an opening some six and a half feet tall and five feet wide.

"Why?" Hunter questioned in a heavy whisper.

"Stinks more than the others," Taylor explained before pointing at an object laying on the floor eight feet into the tunnel. "And that."

Hunter trained his eyes into the tunnel to see a cheap work boot with six inches of what was left of the human leg coming out of it.

"Good bet," Hunter whispered.

"It's gonna be tight," Taylor informed the team. "Single file on my lead. Staggered formation and keep your spacing."

Taylor led his team of five into the tunnel and further into the depths of the earth. The tunnel walls were smooth rock, and the path they walked upon was extremely narrow and littered with signs of activity. In addition to the human foot, the team passed droppings and pools of urine, bones stripped clean of meat, and weathered animal hides dried stiff with the passage of time. The team were silent wraiths cutting the darkness in total invisibility, following the tunnel as it led them further and further away from the main cavern and the human-carved tunnel that brought them to it.

They snaked through the underworld for 30 minutes before the passage opened into a scene torn straight from the nightmares of hell. The cavern was two football fields in size and contained a stagnant lake that covered half that. The sandless beaches were strewn with bones from a dozen different animals and from humans of every size. There were the crushed skulls of infants, collapsed ribcages of adults, and leather that was once human skin or that of animals ripped in half. The team exited the tunnel, stepped into the cavern, and stared through goggles at the signs of a massacre and feeding.

"What the hell is this place?" Nickerson whispered in fearful disbelief.

"Not 'What the hell?'" Drake countered. "This *is* Hell."

33.

"For the love of God!" Ruck barked. "Either speak English or shut up."

Julio stepped back in fear at Ruck's tirade.

Agüera simply laughed.

"What's wrong?" he chided. "Are you feeling left out for not knowing *Española*?"

"Oh yeah," Ruck deadpanned. "I'm sure y'all's conversation over the past 45 minutes has been real life-changing. Y'all solve the problems of the universe, did you?

"Close." Agüera laughed. "No. He was asking me about the United States, and I asked him about digging the tunnel. You know they did all this with picks and shovels and one jackhammer? And that the jackhammer and that generator run on propane?"

"Fascinating." Ruck moaned. "Real sorry I missed out on discussing the intricacies of digging a *narco* tunnel."

"You think you could do it?" Agüera rebutted.

"No," Ruck answered. "Digging holes in the ground wasn't my calling."

"Calling?" Julio interrupted.

"Calling," Agüera began. "It means…"

"It's what you were born to do," Ruck interjected. She held her rifle before her and said, "This is my calling."

Julio nodded in understanding.

"What's your calling, Julio?" Agüera asked.

"I don't know," Julio replied. "We no to get call in Mexico. A man just to do what he to do for he family."

Agüera nodded in agreement.

"Yeah, well, now I got a calling of a different kind," Ruck announced. "Nature's on the horn and she's telling me I gotta take a piss."

"Thanks for the info, babe," Agüera said, chuckling.

"I got your babe right here," Ruck replied with her middle finger.

Agüera smiled and Ruck walked through the passage into the cave. She walked along the wall until she was just outside of the shine from the tunnel's lights. She leaned her rifle against the wall and reached to undo her belt.

The unseen and unheard slammed into her face with such force that it knocked her backward and onto her back. She grabbed the beast in her hands and pressed forward with all her might then heard a sickening crunch as the animal bit through her nose. Pain flashed through her and out her lungs in a primordial scream. The animal ripped into her face was such ferocity that Ruck felt her cheekbones give then shatter. She yanked a handful of fur loose from the beast atop her with her right hand and pulled her pistol from its holster. She jammed the barrel into the animal's side and fired. The blast kicked the animal from her face, and it howled in pain. Ruck scrambled to her feet then put a second round through the animal's head with a scream of anger.

Ruck fell against the wall, grabbed her rifle, then pushed herself back into a standing position. She wiped the blood from her eyes and trained on Agüera who was exiting the tunnel.

34.

Agüera heard the scream.

Then the gunshot.

He slammed Julio against the tunnel wall and down. "Stay here!" he barked.

Agüera ran to the entrance of the cavern, his rifle before him and at the ready. He rushed into the cave to see Ruck stumbling toward him, her face caved in and washed in blood. He started to call her name then saw the horde storm from the darkness.

He saw eight sets of teeth and claws.

Reflective black eyes.

Heard their howling screams of rage.

Agüera raised his rifle and fired.

The beasts were too fast. They slammed Ruck forward into Agüera. Agüera tried to keep his footing but was knocked backward and into the tunnel. He jerked his finger at the impact, unleashing a barrage of gunfire.

Ruck launched herself off of Agüera and rolled over and onto her back. She sloughed the blood from her eyes and fired her pistol into the swarm of baboons overtaking the tunnel. The lead cave dweller leapt outward and came down on her chest. Ruck's arms were hit and her shots went wild. Her second bullet pierced one of the two 100-gallon propane tanks leaning against the wall.

Agüera wrestled himself on top of a baboon and thrust his SOCP dagger into the creature's abdomen. The beast thrust its arms out to fight the pain and inadvertently grabbed the pin of the percussion grenade on Agüera's chest. A smaller monkey leapt onto Agüera's back and slashed and raked the mercenary's head. The beast pulled Agüera's ear from his head, and Agüera shot backward in agony. The sudden jerk of his body and hands completely separated pin from grenade.

35.

Julio watched in terror as the maelstrom of Ruck and Agüera and a pack of beasts exploded into the tunnel. The chaos of gunfire and bullets ricocheting off tunnel walls, screams of pain and the savage will to fight, and the howls of beasts was deafening. Julio heard one of the shots pierce metal then saw and heard the constant expulsion of gas from one of the propane tanks. He watched in shocked disgust as one of the predators ripped Agüera's ear from his head then plunged its claws into the gaping wound it had just created.

Julio started to run then caught the horror in Agüera's eyes at some frightening revelation. Agüera scrambled over his chest, flailing his hands in search of something. A sudden blinding light exploded from beneath Agüera and flashed through the tunnel. Julio went blind. He reached his hands out in front of him then heard the explosion that a nanosecond later sent him hurtling backward and through the air.

36.

"The hell was that?!" Nickerson wildly exclaimed.

"I don't know," Jordan replied. "But I felt it."

The sudden clap of thunder had been followed by a rumble that shook the floor of the cavern and sent ripples across the shallow subterranean lake that Taylor and his team stood before.

"Sounded like…" Hunter began.

"It was an explosion," Taylor insisted. "Sound. Percussion travel differently underground."

Hunter nodded in the darkness.

"It came from the tunnel," Taylor continued.

Hunter got on his radio. "Ruck. Agüera. Come in."

Nothing.

"Ruck. Agüera. Come in."

"I believe this falls to your command," Taylor insisted.

"Team," Hunter commanded in a stern voice. "Back to the tunnel entrance. Taylor's still on point and in command."

"You sure?" Taylor whispered aside to his friend.

"We don't know who or what caused that explosion," Hunter exclaimed. "This down here is your world. Not mine."

Taylor agreed and gave instructions. "Same as before. On me. Staggered positions. Keep your spacing. Double time it."

Taylor turned and led the team back into the narrow tunnel and toward the source of the explosion at a hectic clip.

The team made it back to the cavern in 20 minutes and fanned out after exiting the tunnel with arms ready. They crossed the cavern in haste and took note of the mayhem that had occurred.

Taylor trained in on the fading heat signature of the recently killed baboon. The blood spray from the bullet wound and the pool it created were also glowing with heat.

"Tunnel's closed," Pearce announced. "Something blew the shit out of the entrance. Must be several feet of rock blocking the way in."

"Ruck. Agüera. Come in," Hunter directed into his radio. "Ruck. Agüera. Come in."

"Either they can't reply, or they won't reply," Drake theorized aloud.

"I'm guessing it's can't after this thing came calling," Pearce exclaimed as he kicked the fallen beast in the head.

"We don't know that," Drake rebutted.

"We know Ruck was attacked," Taylor assessed. "And that she didn't fare well."

The team gathered around Taylor and stared at Ruck's torn nose on the cavern floor.

"Guess monkeys don't like nose rings," Nickerson joked.

Drake rushed forward toward Nickerson in writhing anger. Hunter interceded and held her at bay.

"He's free to be an asshole," Hunter barked. "You're not free to clock him for it. Not until we get out of here."

"And just how are we gonna do that?" Pearce inquired from the darkness.

"Again, man, there must be several feet of rock and earth blocking that entrance," Jordan reiterated.

"Juan. Arturo. Come in," Hunter commanded into his radio. "José, come in. José."

"Too much rock between us and them," Taylor explained. "Too much distance."

"So we're not getting through that way," Hunter accepted. "Got any ideas?"

"Drake's monkeys are our best plan," Taylor stated. "Those bones we saw at the lake prove they've been hunting above ground. We find their way out and we'll find our way out."

"That's our best option?" Hunter clarified.

"Yes," Taylor stated. "We can't dig through that rock. We don't have the tools. And even if we could, there's no guarantee our doing so wouldn't make the cave-in worse."

"Then it's down the monkey trail we go," Hunter declared in the darkness.

37.

Miguel burst out of his makeshift office into the barn to Juan, Arturo, José, and the host of other men that stood before the hastily constructed blockade to the tunnel entrance. The men looked at Miguel in fear.

"Well!" Miguel exploded. "Do I have to ask?"

"No boss," Juan cowered.

"Some type of explosion," José reported. "Buckled the door here pretty bad."

"What caused it?" Miguel demanded. "Our men or whoever they found?"

"We don't know," José confessed.

Miguel shot José a look of pure anger at his admittance.

"We've tried reaching them," Juan scrambled. "But all we're getting on the radio is static. There's no answer."

"Keep trying," Miguel commanded.

"You want us to go in there?" Arturo timidly asked.

A look of disbelief washed over Miguel's face. "Do you think you can do better than Hunter and his group?"

"No, sir," Arturo counter. "No, sir, I don't."

"Then stay here and keep trying the radio!"

Miguel turned from his men and walked toward his office. He stopped then turned to face the group he'd just left. "And don't let anything but our men come out of the tunnel. Nothing!"

38.

Agüera's eyes opened.

The world around him was a blur.

His mouth tasted of blood and earth.

His ears were ringing, and his head throbbed in pain.

The ground before him slowly came into view. He saw the glittering jewels of one of his pistol handles lying in a haze of dust. He pulled himself toward it.

But something was wrong.

His body wasn't responding to his will.

Agüera propped himself up with his right arm and looked behind him.

His right leg was gone below the knee.

Agüera's stomach turned. He felt sick. He thought he might vomit. His head was swimming.

Then he heard something.

A low murmur.

Groaning.

Eating noises.

He turned himself completely over and looked beyond his own broken body to see a baboon devouring his severed leg.

The beast made eye contact and dropped Agüera's limb. Agüera turned back over and pulled himself toward his pistol with all his might.

The monkey jumped onto Agüera's back.

It grabbed Agüera's remaining ear.

Agüera pulled himself the last few remaining inches.

The animal opened its jaws and positioned them over Agüera's ear.

Agüera took the pistol in his hand.

The beast bit down.

Agüera screamed.

He thrust the pistol into his open mouth.

And pulled the trigger.

39.

Julio heard the screams somewhere in the back of his subconscious.

He couldn't tell if they were real or if he was dreaming.

The gunshot changed his perspective.

It brought him out of unconsciousness and into the horrifying reality of the tunnel.

Demons in the shape of baboons cackled and howled in the light as they tore and feasted on what was left of Ruck and Agüera. Their bodies were no longer recognizable as humans, replaced instead with shredded parts of what was once whole. One of the beasts held aloft an arm, another sat ripping flesh from a torso, while still another fed at its mother's teat while the source of its milk fished Agüera's eyes from his skull.

The sight was sickening.

Julio gently scooted backward from his position on the ground and toward the tunnel wall. Once there, he slowly stood and held himself flat against the carved earth. He slowly eased his way along the wall, away from the scene of terror.

He moved quietly and deliberately, making each step count and never letting his gaze fall from the animals that he feared. When he could no longer see the monkeys, and knew that they could no longer see him, he broke into a sprint and ran toward the barn entrance as fast as his legs would carry him.

40.

Dejah moved out from under the hole she'd fallen through and frantically brushed the dirt and debris from her hair. The material had fallen upon her shortly after she'd heard what sounded like thunder. The noise was followed by a tremor that shook the ground and sent a shower of filth upon her. Shaking the mess from her hair had sent something into her eye and left her with serious irritation. She wiped her eye repeatedly, but it only made the pain worse.

She decided that she'd try washing the debris from her eye with water from the stream. Dejah couldn't see in the darkness of the cave but knew that if she walked down the incline as she had numerous times earlier that day, she would eventually reach the water. She held her hands out before her and walked slowly in the direction of the stream.

She took small steps and took her time. The cavern was eerily quiet, and she could hear only the shuffling of her feet and the sound of her breathing. She stopped walking when she felt the water on her bare feet. She began to kneel but slipped and fell. She ignored the sudden pain brought on by her collapse and instead cupped her hands to collect water. She washed her eye until the foreign object was flushed free then drank and drank. The water tasted good, but it didn't quell her hunger no matter how much she drank.

Dejah finished drinking and stood. She put her hands out in front of her and shuffled on still wet feet over the cave floor and up the incline. She had walked only a short distance when it occurred to her that she should have been able to see starlight streaming through the hole in the ceiling by now. She shuffled forward and faster in a panic. She stopped and looked above her then all around searching for the faint light that had given her so much hope.

She suddenly wondered if she'd gone the wrong way.

She couldn't have.

Could she have?

She had walked up the incline.

Maybe it was the wrong incline.

Maybe she had walked up the bank on the other side of the stream.

Maybe she had gotten turned around when she fell next to the water.

Dejah tried not to cry.

Not to panic.

She thought for a second and tried to calm herself.

She turned 180° and slowly shuffled forward. She knew this action would take her back to the stream and from there she could go up the other bank and to the hole she so cherished.

She walked and walked, gingerly stepping on bare feet in the direction she felt she was to go.

She felt something moist on her feet and thought perhaps it was moss or algae of some kind but knew for certain that she didn't remember stepping in it before.

She was definitely walking somewhere she'd not walked before.

She knelt and sat, unsure of what to do.

She knew if she continued walking, she'd most likely only get further away from the hole. She thought her best bet was to stay put and wait for the light of day to shine through the hole.

In the meantime, should sit there and wait and try not to cry.

41.

Julio couldn't run anymore.

He was too out of shape and the adrenaline that had given him the strength to come as far as he had had long diminished. He came to a complete stop and fell into a fit of coughing. He buried his head into his arm while doing so in an attempt to muffle the sound. He coughed and coughed then fought to catch his breath then walked onward and toward what he hoped would be salvation.

He wasn't going to let those demon monkeys keep him from a better life with his family in a new country.

Julio thought of this and all the possibilities that awaited him as he kept a steady pace up the tunnel. He reached the point where he'd almost given up dragging his brother when he heard something.

He paused.

He listened.

From the direction he'd escaped came the faint sounds of what sounded like laughing.

Like the horrid sounds of hyenas.

And the chattering of castanets.

The laughter and the clapping increased in pitch.

The noises grew louder.

And closer.

Julio broke into a run. He ran as fast as he could. His lungs were burning. His muscles unable to keep up with this drive. He ran as fast as he could for as long as he could then more.

He coughed.

His body fought for air.

Yet he continued running.

The garage door came into view, giving him a sudden burst of hope that filled his lungs and sped his legs.

He ran forward and slammed into the barricade.

It didn't budge.

He banged the wood with closed fists and screamed for it to be opened.

"Open door!" he cried. "It's Julio. Open door!"

He heard the peals of laughter from before

Whoops.

Howling.

The repetitive clapping of ivory.

Julio turned from the sounds echoing through the tunnel and returned to banging on the barricade.

"Open door!" Julio screamed. "Open the door."

42.

Juan waved his hand to José who was repeating the same message ad nauseam over the radio.

"Cut that shit!" Juan commanded. He took the cigarette from his mouth and tossed it to the ground. He raised his AK-47 to the barrier and stepped back. José, Arturo, and the three other armed men in the barn watched Juan's actions then mirrored them exactly until an army of pistols and rifles were leveled at the heavy wooden structure.

"What?" José whispered.

"Banging," Juan explained in near silence. "Something's banging on the door."

José turned his ear to the structure. "I don't hear...."

The makeshift door exploded outward in a shower of splinters and nails, dust and debris. Julio's bloody, faceless body fell forward into the barn and a swarm of white animals leapt forward. The men screamed in disbelief and fired into the horde.

The cave dwellers pounced upon the men and tore at faces, bit fingers from hands, and pulled ears from heads. Men were knocked about and ended up shooting into one another. Juan accidentally strafed José's body with a half a dozen shots, zipping him from chest to groin. José's body was riveted and danced in spasm then fell to the ground. The sudden shock to his body caused José to fire his AR-15 upward at full auto. Bullets pierced the metal roof and shattered lights. Glass showered down onto the men then fell to the ground only to be painted with the sprayed blood of men and animals.

Arturo fired into the cyclone of violence as he backed away and toward the exit. He unloaded his AK until empty, dropped it, then pulled his 9mm and kept the barrage going as he backed into the hallway. He emptied his pistol into the body of the advancing beast before him and the animal collapsed in death at his feet. Arturo dropped his clip, slammed in another, put one last bullet into the monkey's head, and continued backing down the hall. He came to a door and banged on it while still facing forward.

"Open up, boss!" Arturo commanded. "We're leaving."

The door opened and Miguel pulled Arturo into the room. Arturo slammed the door shut, put his pistol into his waistband, and took the AK-47 that his boss was holding onto for dear life from him. Arturo then kicked the folding conference table over and positioned it in front of the door.

"What the hell is going on out there?!" Miguel demanded.

Arturo went to the far wall behind his boss's desk and unleashed 20 rounds in a horseshoe pattern into and through the exterior wall. Ancient wood splintered outward and the office reverberated in gunfire and in the echo of gunfire. Arturo turned back to face Miguel then jutted his chin in the direction of the corner.

"Boss, the gun."

Miguel nodded then grabbed a second AK-47 from the standing gun rack adjacent to his desk.

The office door shuddered, and Miguel turned to Arturo in search of strength and question. "What's out there?!"

"*Chongos*," Arturo answered in a calm voice. "Lots and lots of pissed off *Chongos*."

Arturo turned back to the wall before him and kicked the shattered boards outward, revealing the darkness of the desert beyond.

The office door shuddered once more and the table that leaned against it fell to the ground. The sounds of howls and screams of anger and excitement grew in volume and permeated through the flimsy door.

"It'll hold 'til I get the car," Arturo promised.

Miguel nodded then fell into sudden shock at the site before him.

A blur of white shot through the newly created opening in the wall and onto the back of Arturo's head. The beast reached around and thrust its claws into Arturo's eyes. Arturo screamed from the deepest well of his being. He dropped his rifle, reached up, and grabbed the violence perched upon him. The cave dweller screamed in seeming delight and pulled Arturo's eyesight from his skull. Arturo pulled a fixed blade knife from his belt and swung wildly above his head in search of purchase.

The animal launched itself off Arturo to Miguel. Miguel raised his rifle and unleashed a torrent of gunfire in responsive panic. The spray went wild with his nervousness and two bullets caught Arturo in the neck. Arturo dropped to his knees in a geyser of arterial spray, painting his surroundings crimson red. The raging animal pounced on my Miguel's chest and knocked him to the ground. Miguel instinctively thrust his arms out to block the creature but was too slow. The animal bit down on Miguel's nose then jerked the severed appendage free and spit it aside. Miguel's howls of pain and fear only seemed to fuel the *papio* onward and into a further frenzy of attack.

The animal slashed Miguel's face open with its claws.

Facial muscles were split in half.

Into thirds.

Bone snapped then collapsed.

Blood pooled, running in every direction and into each new cleave.

Pain surged through Miguel's body, overwhelming his nervous system and his ability to react with emotion or speech.

The animal continued strafing Miguel's face until his eyes dissected into useless slices of collagen fibers.

Miguel's last conscious thought was that of the blissful realization that he didn't have to watch his own death.

43.

Taylor led his team back across the cavern and through the passage to the bank of the subterranean lake.

"It's like déjà vu all over again," Nickerson exclaimed as he panned the cave through night vision goggles.

"Zip it, smartass," Hunter commanded across the darkness.

Taylor ignored Nickerson and Hunter's cross talk and surveyed the scene before him for a second time.

He studied the lake and its shore, the cave ceiling and its walls. He inventoried ridges of karst and rimstone and made note of the temperature and heavy humidity. He visually measured how far the remains of fallen man and beast lay from the shore and the depth of the footsteps and claw marks that surrounded them. He counted four passages that were large enough to serve as entrances to the caverns, as well as exits from the underworld. Taylor led the team around the lake to the first passage. He studied it through thermal goggles and found some signs of usage. The second and third passages showed sign as well. But the fourth was by far the most widely used. It held the trickle of a stream and was littered with prints of caked mud, shed fur, discarded bone, and foodstuff. It smelled of musk and putrid urine.

"This is the one," Taylor whispered.

The team stood in a half-moon formation around the passage entrance and watched as Taylor explained his findings.

"They've been using all these passages," Taylor continued. "But this one by far the most. My bet is that it will eventually lead up and out."

The team nodded in agreement.

"How we gonna fit?" Pearce exclaimed, noting the tunnel's height of just over five foot.

"You'll just have to turn hunchback for a time," Hunter joked.

"It might open up to something taller," Taylor offered, ignoring the comments from Pearce and Hunter. "So, until then, it's heads down and take the problems as they come."

The team nodded in the affirmative once more.

Taylor ducked his head and partially hunched over. He held his rifle at the ready and entered the tight, narrow passage. The team followed in single file, each adapting to the confines of the passage in their own fashion.

The floor of the passage was slick rock and worn smooth by the flow of water over a period of time no one knew. The air was thick with humidity and made hot by some unknown means. Taylor led his team through the passage and around and through the small stream and the narrow pools it formed. Occasionally, they passed the remains of some animal discarded or washed onto the rock shore and footprints of primates left in silt or loose gravel.

The passage slowly widened and the ceiling rose. The team came to a small chamber that allowed them to gather around each other for the first time since they entered the tunnel some 45 minutes earlier. They paused to stretch their backs from the strain of being bent for so long and checked or changed the batteries in their goggles. Some took the opportunity to smoke and others to drink water or to eat.

"Some crazy shit down here," Hunter noted to Taylor on an exhale of cigarette smoke. He held his pack of cigarettes out before him, and Taylor took one and lit it.

"Yeah, I never would've guessed my introduction to the job would involve discovering a new species," Taylor dryly observed on a puff of smoke.

"Discovered it and, if things go right, blast it into extinction," Hunter joked.

The men paused to enjoy their smokes and further stretch their backs.

"Where you think they came from?" Hunter began again.

Taylor took a long drag on his cigarette then offered, "Zoo. Carnival maybe. Long time ago."

"A zoo!" Hunter exclaimed in humorous disagreement. "They got out of a zoo then decided to live in a hole? Underground? That doesn't make any sense."

"Shit, Hunter. I don't know. And I really don't care." Taylor laughed. "You asked and I said the first thing that came to my mind."

"Huh. That was the first thing that came to your mind?" Hunter smirked. He dropped his cigarette butt and moved to grind it into the ground with his boot then kicked it to the side into the half-inch deep creek to his right instead. "Because the first thing that usually comes to my mind is porn."

"Even when talking about monkeys?" Taylor laughed.

"Especially. You'd be amazed at the sexual shit a monkey can do when put before a camera and properly directed."

The two men stood silent for a bit then burst into laughter.

44.

Taylor called an end to the break then led the team forward and into the next section of the tunnel. The passage opened up and the team was no longer forced to walk with their backs hunched over or bent to either side. The passage also widened but not so much that they could hike side-by-side. They maintained a single-file line and followed the passage and the intermittent stream within it, all the while watching for sign of exit or for more of the animals that had begun their mission so far under the earth.

Taylor brought the team to a sudden halt with a raised clenched fist. The team stopped and then followed Taylor into a crouch and made themselves ready for whatever was to come. Taylor called Hunter to his side with the motion of his hand then pointed to an object some 100 yards before them. Hunter studied the signature then shrugged his shoulders to inform Taylor that he had no idea what the object was.

Taylor called Drake and Nickerson forward and led them and Hunter out of the passage. They entered into a vast cavern much larger and taller than the one that served as the beginning of their journey. They moved forward and toward the object like wraiths, spectral mercenaries focused only on the single object before them. They covered 20 yards then came to a stop and studied the object from a stationary position. Taylor stared hard at the heat signature. It was considerably larger than the dead baboon they'd examined but pretty much the same shape. Taylor didn't notice a tail but then he wasn't sure if monkey tails carried as much heat as the rest of their bodies.

Or if all the monkeys in the cave system had tails.

Taylor led the team closer. They covered another 20 yards in near silence and with swift determination. Taylor brought the team once more to a halt then studied the figure from a closer distance.

The heat signature was sitting with legs spread out before it and its arms held at its side.

Monkeys didn't sit like that.

Did they?

No.

It was a child.

Taylor's mind flashed through 1,000 questions at once.

What would a child be doing down here?

Was it along?

Had it been abandoned?

How could he approach it in total darkness without frightening it?

Taylor turned to the team and whispered, "It's a kid."

"Just about to say that," Hunter offered. "But didn't want to sound crazy before you did. What the hell's a kid doing down here?"

"That kid damn near got lit up!" Nickerson exclaimed, lowering his rifle.

"It can't see or hear us and the last thing I want to do is scare it," Taylor explained.

"You don't think it's already scared being down here in a cave?" Nickerson interrupted.

Taylor ignored the comment and instead turned to Drake. "Your voice will be the least frightening."

"Why because I'm a woman?"

"Yes," Taylor answered.

"Screw that," Drake snapped. "I'm supposed to like kids because I'm a woman?"

"I don't care if you like them or not," Taylor shot back. "I'm talking about your voice."

"I hate kids. I won't even watch my niece's kids. They're brats."

Taylor sighed and stood. He called across the darkness in as calm a voice as he could muster. "Hello. My name is Taylor."

Dejah turned to the call in shock and fright. She was both elated and scared to death. She stood and called back across the black ink. "Where are you? Who are...?"

"I'm about 60 yards away."

Dejah scanned the darkness as though she would be able to see. "I can't see you," she called.

"But I can see you," Taylor replied in his friendliest voice. "I'm with three other people and we're wearing special glasses that allow us to see in the dark."

"Is my mom with you?"

Taylor heard the fear and uncertainty in the girl's voice. He gathered the girl had been separated from her mother somehow and was scared and alone. The sight of soldiers with guns and crazy goggles would only scare her even more so. He wanted to do anything he could to avoid that.

"We're gonna walk over to you, okay?" Taylor called.

"What about my mother? What about Carlos?"

Taylor continued to politely ignore the child and instead walked his team forward. When they were within 10 yards, Taylor brought them to a standstill and ordered them through his commentary with the girl.

"What's your name?

"Dejah."

"Dejah. That's a pretty name. Dejah, my friends and I are soldiers. We have guns…"

"Are you the Border Patrol?"

Hunter laughed at the idea.

Taylor continued. "No, Dejah, we're soldiers. Now we're gonna turn on our flashlight so you can see us and we can better see you."

Dejah started shaking in fear and anticipation.

She was scared.

And scared of what was to come.

Taylor turned on his flashlight and the others followed.

Dejah looked at the faces of the men and one woman and watched them as they held their distance.

They weren't scary at all.

45.

The team assembled around Dejah and gave her food and water. They gave her a glow stick that shined neon green once it was snapped and shaken and she wore it around her neck on a necklace made of cord and tied into a loop by Taylor. Nickerson looked at Dejah's ankle and the scrapes, cuts, and bruises that covered most of her body and declared, "She'll live."

"Christ, you're worse with kids then I am," Drake scoffed.

"What?!" Nickerson countered. "Told her she'll live. That's nice."

The team listened to Dejah as she answered questions of how she came to be where she was and of how she got even more lost when she went for water. Dejah explained that she spoke English as well as she did because her mother was a school teacher and had been teaching her English all her life in anticipation of them moving to the United States. Dejah said that the journey thus far had been long and difficult but that she never thought it would end up as it had. She detailed how the earth had given way underneath her and how she had fallen through it and how she'd heard screams from above after she had come to be in the cavern. She told about the blood and fingers that rained down on her and how it had scared her like nothing had ever scared her before. The team nodded in understanding and complimented her on her English and how well she spoke and how brave she had been.

Hunter and Nickerson left the team in the glow of the flashlights to look for the hole that Dejah had entered the cavern through.

"Hole can't be that high above us," Hunter mused. "If all she did was hurt her ankle on the way down, it couldn't have been that much of a fall."

Taylor agreed and watched him and Nickerson leave then returned his attention back to Dejah.

"So other than the hole you fell through, have you seen any other light?" Taylor asked. "Lanterns or flashlights? Matches? Sunlight maybe?"

Dejah nodded in the affirmative. "I saw some light. I guess from holes above me. That's how I found the water. There was light shining down on it."

"A lot of light?"

Dejah shook her head. "No. Just a little. Smaller than your flashlight."

"The beam? You mean smaller than the beam it puts out?"

"Yes, smaller than the flashlight beam."

Taylor nodded and smiled. He continued, "Before I called to you, had you heard from anyone else? Heard anyone talking or yelling way off in the distance maybe?"

"No. The only thing I heard from way off was those dogs."

"Dogs?" Drake interrupted.

"Yes. Dogs," Dejah reiterated.

"Did you see them?" Taylor began anew.

"No. I only heard them."

"What did they sound like?" Taylor continued.

"They were far away," Dejah recounted. "But they sounded angry. Like they were mean dogs. They growled and had really loud barks."

"What did you do when you heard them?"

"I got scared," Dejah admitted. "So, I got real quiet. I didn't want them to hear me."

For the first time since his daughter's death, Taylor reached out and touched another person with fatherly compassion. His gently placing his hand on Dejah's shoulder was a sign of care and understanding, of the need and the desire to offer protection and safety, and of parental feelings and guidance.

"That kid is lucky to be alive," Hunter exclaimed from a short distance away. "She must've dropped 18 to 20 feet."

"Can we get out that way?" Taylor asked, standing to meet his friend.

"No. That crack she fell through is too small for any of us to get through. Kinda surprised she fit."

"Then we will just have to find another way out," Taylor promised.

Dejah looked up at Taylor and smiled.

46.

Jared and others in his research party sat in a circle around the remains of the previous night's fire. The group drank beer or plastic cups of wine, joking and laughing as they enjoyed the cooler temperatures that evening brought and gazing in wonderment at the stars. The group discussed their day in the cave, their findings, and what it would mean to the area and to the university they were each associated with. Dr. Cooke offered praise to all those involved in the day's dig and that they were working so well together. He also commented on speculation about what would be found in the sinkhole in the weeks to come.

Jared interrupted the praise to belch loudly. Most in the group laughed while others feigned shock or disappointment.

"Sorry," Jared apologized. "Warm beer does that to me. Speaking of, is anyone making a supply run tomorrow 'cause I'm in serious need of some ice."

"Why don't you ask your monkeys to fetch you some?" Angie joked across the stone-cold fire pit.

"Ha. Ha. Ha," Jared both said and belched. "I said that it smelled like monkey shit down there. I didn't say there were any monkeys down there."

"The idea that you even considered it, monkeys in a cave, let alone in Texas is crazy," Angie continued goading.

"No. It's not," Jared countered. "Monkeys in Texas is actually a thing and they do quite well."

The group stared across the twilight to Jared in disbelief.

Jared saw this, exhaled a heavy sigh, and explained. "So, this married couple over in Dilley, near San Antonio, put 150 Japanese snow monkeys on their ranch back in the early nineties…"

"Why?!" Aubrey scoffed.

"Because they liked monkeys, I guess," Jared speculated. "Anyway, monkeys being monkeys, they started going at it and soon there was over 600 of these nasty red-faced and skank-assed vermin running around the property."

"Skank-assed vermin," Angie mocked. "And you're a scientist?"

"Oh yeah. Hell yeah I'm a scientist," Jared exclaimed. He killed his beer, dropped the bottle, and edged forward in his camp chair. "So, there's over 600 monkeys at this ranch and then the owners of the ranch get divorced and while they're hashing it out in court, the ranch goes abandoned and the electric fence went down, and the monkeys went bye-bye. But the thing is that their numbers actually increased outside of the enclosure. They did that well in the south Texas scrublands."

"Then how come south Texas isn't overrun with monkeys?" Angie asked.

"Deer hunters mostly," Jared replied.

"Deer hunters what?" Angie followed.

"Deer hunters shot 'em," Jared explained.

"That's terrible," Angie almost sobbed. "Why? Why would they do such a thing?"

"I dunno. They're out there in the wilds. Have a rifle. See a monkey. Bam!"

Angie started to openly weep and Tom took her place in the question and answer session with Jared. "So, you think some of these monkeys went down in the hole. They defecated in it and that's why it smells like monkey shit? Is that right?"

"I never said that," Jared clarified. "I just said it smelled like monkey shit down there. I don't know if any of those Dilley, Texas monkeys made it down there or if another group of monkeys was down there or if any monkeys were ever down there at all. But it does smell like monkey shit down there."

47.

Megan had heard enough about monkeys and monkey shit. She was hot and tired and felt the coming of a migraine, and sitting out under the stars was doing nothing to change that. She finished her plastic cup of wine and leaned over to tell Tom she was going to bed.

"Do you want me to come with you?" Tom sheepishly asked.

"Are you tired?" Megan asked, missing Tom's true intentions.

"No, but I want to go to bed with you."

Megan rolled her eyes, mumbled, "Give it up," and bid goodnight to all around the fireless fire pit.

"You want me to at least walk you to the tent?"

"Tom. Seriously. Give it up," Megan growled in annoyance.

Tom chuckled and Megan assured him she could make it to their tent just fine on her own. She left the circle and brought her flashlight to life. She walked down the narrow trail and past the other tents to the one she shared with Tom. She lay on top of her sleeping bag and closed her eyes, hoping that relief from all her ailments and problems would come quickly.

48.

Jared had walked away from the group in the opposite direction as Megan. He walked away without the aid of a flashlight, instead utilizing the stars and moon to illuminate the path before him. He rounded a small stand of mesquite trees then stood at its edge to urinate. He had just finished when he heard the faintest of sounds.

Or was it the absence of sounds?

Regardless, something caught his attention.

Something out of the ordinary.

He zipped his fly and strained to listen for some sign or indication of his sudden and unexpected sense of unease. He turned away from the stand of mesquite to face the small clearing before him. He scanned a tangle of brush circling the packed-earth opening then jumped at the sight of the creature hidden just within a spider web of cactus, thorn-covered vines, and skeletal limbs.

The animal was small, not much larger than a house cat. It was bone white yet somehow well camouflaged among the shadows. It sat on rear legs and held itself sturdy among the vegetation with what were clearly hands.

Jared moved gingerly toward the animal then fished a small penlight from his pocket. He shined the light toward the well-hidden animal then watched as it shielded its eyes with its hands. The creature hissed in response to the brightness of the light revealing a maw of canine teeth.

"What are you?" Jared rhetorically asked aloud, still trying to get a full picture of the small animal.

The creature hissed once more and was then echoed by a louder, deeper hiss.

Jared turned slowly to his left to witness the source of the vocalization.

The curiosity before him was enormous, standing over two feet at the shoulder and weighing perhaps 100 pounds. Despite the faint light, Jared could tell the grayish white beast was well-muscled.

And aggravated.

The creature tilted its head as if in study then released a guttural growl of fury.

The beast eased forward.

Jared stepped back.

A mesquite branch poked him in the shoulder.

He turned to see what it was.
Turning his back to the animal was the last mistake he ever made.

49.

Dr. Cooke was waxing poetic way about the latest published findings on mastodons in Texas when his group heard the scream. Everyone jumped at the sudden shrill and sat in nervous fear at the unexplained until Tom broke the silence by yelling into the darkness, "Knock it off, Jared!"

Some in the group laughed at the command while others held their chests as if the action would slow their heart rate or allow them to catch their breath. Those that had laughed fell into silence at the sound of brush rustling. All eyes converged in the direction of the disturbance and the group watched as the vegetation violently parted to reveal a haunting figure stumbling forward.

What was left of Jared ambled into view. His eyes were gone, replaced with torn red flesh, his face a mosaic of deep cuts, flayed skin, and streaks of blood. The resemblance of their friend held his throat in tightly gripped hands in an attempt to quell the flow of blood pouring forth from some unseen cut or cuts.

A female in the group screamed in terror at the sight. Some stood in shock or disbelief. Tom stepped forward then stopped in the realization that there was nothing he could do for the man standing before him at the precipice of death. Jared's body collapsed forward and again a female in the group shrilled in terror at the scene unfolding where the human form once stood.

More than a dozen primates, each the color of bleached bone and recently painted in splattered blood, stood at the edge of the brush. The smallest of the group came forward and on top of Jared's fallen body. The creature tore a softball-sized chunk of flesh from Jared's neck and begin feeding upon it. Dr. Cooke started to yell or to vocalize something in protest or in shock but was unable to before the remaining beasts sprung forward in attack.

The fire ring exploded into a melee of rampage and violence, of predator and prey, survival and agonizing death. The cave dwellers pounced and thrashed, tore and ravaged in an all-out assault to disable then devour their quarry.

Tom was of the few to not allow his previous life of relative ease to dictate his death. He sprung from his chair at the sight of the mob and kicked his attacker in the head as it lunged at him. The beast flew sideways and into a camp chair. Monkey and chair tumbled and rolled as if one then came to a stop in a twist of animal, aluminum, plastic, and fabric. Tom watched as the nylon seat of the chair shredded outward. He grabbed an empty beer bottle and smashed it over the dog-like snout that fought through the chair. He pulled back the remains of the bottle then thrust the now spear-tipped longneck into the creature's neck and twisted. The still-imprisoned animal flailed and screamed then fell silent.

Tom rose to his feet only be tackled from behind. He fell forward and into the chair and shards of broken glass. He ignored the pain of the fall and of the fragments of broken bottle embedded in his cheek and tried to right himself. The animal that had knocked him forward pounced onto his upper back and begin clawing its way through Tom's neck, scalp, and the sides of his face. Tom pushed off the ground with all his strength. The animal clung to his back, driving his claws into his body deeper and deeper in search of purchase. Tom stood and reached behind him to try to dislodge his attacker.

Tom caught the baboon's right forearm in his grip. The baboon howled in surprise, arched back and away from Tom's body, then plunged into his neck with canine teeth. Tom screamed and fought then fell silent at the sound of bone snapping. His body went numb at the breaking of his spine. He collapsed to the ground in a heap, his body now useless and beyond his control. He scanned the fire ring with stationary eyes looking for signs of help, listening in horror as the animal fed upon him.

50.

Megan was a heavy sleeper so waking up because of a noise was a new experience for her. At first, she thought she dreamed the screaming but now that she was alert and sitting up, she knew the cries were real. She thought the gathering she had left had gotten out of hand, that maybe folks had drank too much and we're now acting foolish or perhaps fighting. This theory faded quickly as the screams became interspersed with the cries and snarls of animals. She thought the vocalizations were from dogs but then believed they were from something else. The barks and howls were too deep for dogs, at least any of the kind of dogs she knew of.

The human cries, however, were unmistakable.

They were sounds of fear and anger and reminded her of a cheap horror movie. Megan's mind raced through ideas of what to do in response to what she was hearing. Her first instinct was one that a child might have: to hide, to climb under the covers and hope and pray the scenario away. Maturity pushed this idea behind her and replaced it with the idea to attempt to help.

Or to flee.

She quickly put on a pair of jeans and unlaced boots and crawled out of the tent. She turned on her phone and shielded the light of the screen with cupped hands to see that she had no signal. She shoved the phone into her pocket and listened to her surroundings. The cacophony of sounds changed in tune.

Gone were the harrowing screams of pain and death, replaced instead with the sounds of lapping and tearing. She edged down the trail toward the fire pit, keeping to the side of the trail, trying to let the brush partially shield her body from sight. She came to a stop behind a small clump of huisache trees and peered through their tangle of branches to the source of the noise some 10 yards beyond the vegetation. She saw fallen bodies being torn apart, reduced to meat and pools of blood and being fed upon by animals unlike any she'd seen before. She covered her mouth with clasped hands to stifle her scream and the feeling that she would be sick.

The closest animal to her stood from the carrion it fed upon and barked in her direction. She didn't know if the action was directed at her or if the creature saw her but she ran in response to it. She ran with full abandon down the trail, past her tent, and into the brush. Thorns from limbs and vines scratched at her skin and snagged and pulled at her shirt and jeans. She ran through cobwebs and over rocks and skirted cactus. She ran as fast as she could, never looking back, always looking forward. She ran until she felt her lungs would burst then ran some more until it was physically impossible for her to do so. She fell to her knees in exhaustion at the edge of a dead cedar and fought to catch her breath. She crawled behind the tree and looked to the area she'd just fled. She saw nothing but a landscape of harsh realities painted in faint moonlight.

The sight made her weep.

51.

Taylor and the rest of his team had gone through a long list of ideas on how to deal with Dejah's lack of shoes but in the end decided she'd just have to walk barefoot. If the group encountered too rough of a terrain, the team would take turns carrying her until she could walk again. The team had also discussed the best way to deal with her lack of night or thermal vision.

"We can tie a rope around her," Drake suggested.

"Like a leash?!" Nickerson scarfed. "Jesus, girl. You really don't like kids, do you?"

"So, we should all just hold hands then?" Drake countered.

"We'll use flashlights," Taylor decreed. "We'll rotate through usage to conserve batteries."

"Do you think we're going to be down here that much longer?" Pearce asked.

"No," Taylor responded. "I doubt those monkeys…"

"Agartha baboons," Drake corrected. "I named 'em, I get to enforce proper name usage."

"I doubt these monkeys…" Taylor continued.

"Really?" Drake jokingly barked.

Taylor smirked and continued.

"I don't think Drake's new species would travel too far underground to get to a hunting area. There's bound to be multiple entrances to down here. We'll find one soon."

"Then let's get to it," Hunter exclaimed. "Let's get back to the top. That beer don't drink itself."

"And find my mom," Dejah both interrupted and reminded.

Taylor looked to the child and the innocence and hope she wore upon her face.

"Gonna do our best," Taylor promised.

Dejah smiled and stood, watching as the team gathered their gear, tightened their straps, and made themselves at the ready. Taylor led them along the tiny stream in the cavern until it disappeared into a crack in the wall. He skirted the wall and soon found a tunnel he believed was the one animals had been using then sighed at the size of the passage.

"Another tight one," Nickerson complained.

Taylor nodded.

"You sure this is the one?" Nickerson continued.

Taylor studied the ground inside and out of the tunnel and said, "Afraid so."

Taylor eased into the five-foot-tall by three-foot-wide passage and shined his light forward and into the void.

"Looks like it opens up again in 'bout 20 yards or so," Taylor announced from just inside the tunnel. "We're just gonna have to hunchback it again."

Dejah walked into the tunnel and next to Taylor.

"I only have to tilt my head down a little bit," she observed.

"Blessed are the short." Pearce laughed.

A few in the group chuckled then returned to silence as Taylor led them into the cramped passage. The going was difficult, and it took them almost a half hour to cover a distance of almost 20 yards. There, the passage opened up slightly to reveal a split in the tunnel, as well as a shaft that went straight up.

Taylor, Hunter, Drake, and Dejah cramped together under the shaft and studied the sides of the chimney with their flashlights.

"They've been going up that way," Taylor decreed before turning his attention back to ground level. "And down both these tunnels."

Hunter wiped the sweat from his brow then spit and said, "Which tunnel down here 'cause we ain't climbing up that thing. We don't have the gear and even if we did, Drake and the kid here would be the only ones that could fit."

Taylor returned his gaze to the split before him. He peered into each of the passages in study then declared that the smaller of the two was the correct avenue.

Hunter nodded in his friend's direction and announced, "You heard the man. Let's go."

Given the confines of the tunnel, all but Dejah had to walk sideways and lean over or to the side to maneuver through the passageway. The progress they made was extremely slow and all were annoyed at where they found themselves.

"God damn do it smell in here!" Nickerson complained. "Like straight up ammonia."

"Animal piss," Drake corrected.

"What?" Nickerson countered.

"The ammonia smell," Drake explained. "It's animal piss."

"From your monkeys?" Nickerson continued.

"Most likely," Drake offered. "And that smell is most likely why Taylor here chose this tunnel. Am I right?"

Taylor ignored the question directed at him and instead announced in a heavy whisper, "Big cave up ahead. Maybe five yards."

Taylor led the group through the arduous task of moving forward until the tunnel gave way to a vast opening. He stepped out from the tunnel and cast his flashlight beam outward and to the interior. What he saw shattered his stoic demeanor and sent a shiver up his spine.

"My God," he whispered.

52.

Megan hadn't moved in hours. She had sat behind the shelter of the cedar tree in isolated fear. The first sign of dawn gave her some but even there, in the growing light, she was still frightened of what she'd seen and of what she feared might come.

As the light grew, she came to realize that she wasn't actually that far from camp. She couldn't see the camp, any of the tents or vehicles, but could see in the distance the scrub oak tree that she and Tom had camped under. This realization turned her thoughts to Tom.

Was he still alive?

Still there in the area of the fire pit?

Was he hurt and unable to move?

Or was he dead like those she had seen?

She didn't want to think about the latter.

The sun continued to rise, bringing with it the Texas heat and a better view of the landscape between her and camp. Megan stood, stretched, and slowly made her way through the brush that she had plowed through the night before toward camp. She stopped at her tent and crawled inside. She downed a half liter of water and ate a granola bar. She exited the tent and moved cautiously toward camp. She had almost reached the tree that she'd hid behind the night before when a small kit fox darted through the brush before her. She jumped back from the sight and grabbed her chest in fright. She paused a moment to collect herself then walked the remaining distance to the tree from where she'd seen the massacre.

The sight she witnessed beyond the branches she stood safely behind was horrifying. There were bodies and pieces of bodies everywhere. The ground was soaked with blood and the area was already swarming with flies. The faces of the human dead had been mangled and torn beyond recognition, and the clothing that could have identified the remains were shredded and cast aside. Megan put her hand to her mouth and pulled it away as fast as she could and retched. She wiped her mouth with the back of her hand and then wiped away the tears streaming from her eyes with the other.

She circled the brush that surrounded the fire pit, trying not to see any more of the hellish landscape that it had become, and made her way to the path that led to the clearing where the vehicles were parked. She climbed into the cab of Tom's truck, locked the door behind her, and sobbed. She banged the steering wheel with gripped fists and screamed then calmed herself enough to think.

She opened the center consul and dug Tom's keys from the mess within, brought the truck to a roar, and punched the gas.

53.

Taylor studied the cave in disbelief.

He ignored the team as they pried themselves from the tunnel behind him and instead shined a light over and up the walls of the cave, noting the multiple ledges, the grass and limbs strewed upon them, and the honeycomb of passages that led in almost every direction.

"What the…?"

Taylor didn't let Hunter finish.

"Nests," Taylor declared. "This is where they've been bedding down. This is their home."

"Or one of them," Drake added. She too was staring at the latticework of bedding areas. "We don't know how many troops live down here."

"Troops?" Pearce asked.

"Baboons travel in troops," Drake explained. "In groups as small as five to groups of over 200 in number."

"Two hundred?!" Nickerson exclaimed in disbelief. "I ain't got but maybe 150 rounds."

"Like you'd be the only one shooting them." Jordan laughed.

Nickerson's and Jordan's joking was interrupted by a shrill bark.

The team swung around to see a fawn-colored baboon perched upon a ledge some 15 feet up. The monstrosity growled and stomped its front feet in anger. Taylor raised his AR until the green laser sight upon it projected a small dot on the beast's head and squeezed the trigger. The baboon's head exploded outward in a spray of red and gray matter. The rifle's report echoed across the cavern, and the animal fell to the floor below with a resounding thud. The team surrounded the oddity and Dejah pushed forward for a closer view of the dead animal.

"Back away from it, honey," Taylor warned.

"Awwwww," Dejah cooed. "It's a monkey."

The cavern suddenly exploded into a symphony of violent screams and howls. Dozens of baboons appeared on ledges, in pockmarks in the walls, and in the entrances to other tunnels.

"Playtime, motherfuckers!" Nickerson roared as he unleashed a torrent of gunfire toward a wall climbing with monkeys.

"Behind me!" Taylor screamed as he grabbed Dejah by the shoulder and flung her behind him.

"Nickerson. Pearce. Jordan," Hunter commanded. "Your three and six. Taylor, Drake, and I have nine and noon."

The team split down the middle to cover their respective areas and released a barrage of gunfire at the advancing primates.

The cave reverberated with gunfire and danced in the strobe lighting of semi- and full-auto muzzle flashes. Green sighting lasers pierced the darkness and traced across the cavern in search of targets.

"Lights!" Taylor screamed over the melee. "Lights on! Blind them!"

Flashlights ignited and the beams they projected pierced the darkness.

Dejah fell to her knees and covered her ears, screaming in confusion and complete fear.

The baboons were too many and too fast.

They zigzagged through the darkness, dancing around gunfire, jetting in and out of the light, and under and over sighting lasers.

A monstrous bull baboon weighing well over 120 pounds plowed out of the darkness and into Nickerson's chest, knocking him to the ground. The sudden blow caused Nickerson to strafe his rifle upward as he fell. The animal came to rest on Nickerson's chest and violently slashed at his face and neck with talon-like claws. Nickerson pulled his knife from its sheath on his flak jacket and plunged it into the creature's side. The animal howled in surprise and pain. It reared back in agony then attacked Nickerson's neck with berserker speed and tenacity. Nickerson pulled his knife from his attacker's side then stabbed it into the beast's flesh once more. The baboon shrilled then ripped Nickerson's trachea from his throat. Nickerson grabbed what was left of his neck to feel his life pouring forth.

Pearce rushed to his fallen comrade with machete in hand. Pearce swung the blade into and through the primate's neck, decapitating the animal. Nickerson smiled in response to the action then faded into darkness.

A mob of eight baboons of many sizes surrounded Pearce. He brought his machete blade down and into the skull of the first animal. The beast wobbled then collapsed with the short sword still lodged in its head. Pearce raised his rifle and fired into the remaining seven animals, dropping two and wounding another three. The smallest of the remaining group leapt for Pearce's face only to land at the end of his rifle barrel instead. Pearce jerked the trigger and the animal was almost halved by the blast, falling to the ground in two barely connected pieces.

Another animal made it to Pearce's face. Pearce wobbled backward at the impact. He pulled the creature from his face by the scruff of its back and slammed it to the ground. He stepped on the beast's neck, dropped his rifle to point blank against the animal's face, and shot it. Pearce raised up to enter the fight once more but was overrun by three baboons that launched themselves into his chest all at once. Pearce was knocked to the ground and the baboons combined on his face and neck with such tenacious force that it ensured he would never rise again.

54.

Taylor didn't have to give the command.

Didn't have to say a word.

Hunter and Drake were well aware of the situation and they understood its gravity.

Their team was being overrun.

The attack that had begun with a single animal, turned into a charge by a few dozen, was now an overwhelming, marauding force of more than 50 animals. The scourge had taken out Nickerson, devoured Pearce, and was currently taking the last bit of life from Jordan.

"That one!" Taylor exclaimed over the frantic turmoil, pointing with his chin to a tunnel to his right.

Hunter and Drake responded with actions rather than words.

They fired into the wave of attackers as they pivoted with Taylor and Dejah into a slow retreat toward the exit.

"Out!" Drake ripped, letting her rifle hang at her side by its sling. She pulled her pistol, grabbed Dejah, and led the child into the passage. The tunnel was larger than the last few passages had been at almost seven feet high and was wide enough to allow Drake and Dejah to stand side-by-side with no issue.

"Reloading!" Hunter yelled over the rampage to Taylor.

"Into the tunnel!" Taylor countered. "Go!"

Hunter entered the tunnel and dropped the magazine from his AR. He slapped another one in, chambered a round, and made his way to Drake and Dejah who stood just a few feet inside the passage.

"Where's Taylor?" Dejah questioned in fear.

"He's coming," Hunter assured the little girl.

"Good, 'cause I've got something for his friends," Drake said, swinging the flamethrower from her pack.

Hunter cracked a smile and covered the entrance to the tunnel.

Taylor backed into the passage, still firing at the unseen outside the tunnel.

"Go!" Taylor commanded, looking over his shoulder. "Go!"

Hunter, Drake, and Dejah barreled forward and down the tunnel. Taylor backed further into the passage firing as he went.

"How far?" Taylor asked into his radio.

"Twenty-five yards in and waiting," Hunter replied over the radio.

Taylor backed further down the passage, firing at the hostiles before him as he did. He pulled an M84 stun grenade from his tactical vest, armed it, and tossed it before him. Baboons swarmed into the passage. Taylor fired thrice more then ran down the tunnel. The animals followed. The lead primate came to a halt at the thrown circular object on the ground and smelled the area.

The sudden detonation of the grenade unleashed a blinding wave of seven million candela and the percussion of 170 decibels.

The tunnel shook, and loose earth and gravel on the floor jumped.

55.

Hunter pulled Dejah close to him and said, "Get ready."

Dejah nodded and held tight to Hunter's waist. She closed her eyes and took a deep breath. She heard the explosion and then felt the faint remains of the shockwave as it traveled down the tunnel and into her, Hunter, and Drake. Dejah opened her eyes and asked, "Is that it? It's over?"

Hunter ignored the question, gently pushed Dejah off of him, and got into a crouched position with his rifle pointed before him.

He raised from this position only a moment later when he saw Taylor jogging toward him.

"Never get used to just how loud those things are, do you?" Hunter joked.

Taylor stuck his fingers in his ears then laughed. "Huh?"

"All gone?" Drake asked Taylor.

"Doubt it," Taylor admitted.

"Nothing at our six," Drake continued.

"Then let's go that way," Taylor said.

"But is it a way out?" Drake queried.

Taylor walked past Hunter, Drake, and Dejah and further into the tunnel. He studied the floor and walls with the aid of his flashlight. He saw evidence of plenty of comings and goings on the primates' part, and he explained such to the remainder of his team. He took point and led Hunter, Drake, and Dejah further into the passage and away from the carnage behind them.

56.

"Buzzards," Agent Andrews announced from behind his binoculars. "A whole bunch of them."

"You mean flock," Agent Carter countered from behind his own pair of binoculars.

The two agents were standing atop the roof of their SUV, studying the early morning sky. Agent Carter turned to face the same direction as Andrews and reiterated his coworker's earlier declaration.

"Yep, that's one big flock."

Agent Andrews lowered his binoculars and turned to Agent Carter.

"I used the collective noun 'bunch' because we're in a casual setting and as such formality is not required."

"I understand," Agent Carter countered. "I was only trying to help you."

"Then you should have corrected me with 'wake,' as it's the correct collective noun for buzzards," Agent Andrews corrected. "Also acceptable are 'venue' or 'kettle.'"

"Kettle? Really?"

"Yes. And venue."

"I had no idea."

"Now you know."

The two men ceased their discussion of buzzards and the collective nouns associated with the birds and stood upon the roof in silence studying the area surrounding them. A sudden cloud of dust on the road below the circling buzzards caught their eye. They trained their binoculars on the abnormality and Agent Andrews asked aloud, "What is that?"

57.

Megan was hysterical.

All that she had seen and heard had caught up with her and flooded her body with pain, fear, and uncertainty.

She sobbed uncontrollably.

Screamed at things in the truck.

And cursed the road before her.

The biggest problem with the latter was the ruts and potholes that kept her from driving faster.

The second was the caliche dust that kicked up from before Tom's truck and coated it in talcum.

"Shit! Shit! Shit!" she screamed through heavy sobs. "Shit! Shit! Shit!"

Megan flipped the truck's windshield wipers on and flooded the windshield with washer fluid. The powder-like dust mixed with washer fluid and frosted the windshield in a white-colored sludge. Megan continued cursing and pumped the windshield washer until the control wand broke off in her hand.

The wipers opened a hole in the sludge just in time for Megan to clearly see the Border Patrol vehicle she was about to plow into at 50 miles per hour.

58.

Agent Andrews and Agent Carter jumped off the roof of their vehicle just as it was struck by the speeding truck. Both men rolled off the ground and instinctively rose to their feet with sidearms drawn. They cautiously approached the wrecked vehicle, cutting through a cloud of radiator steam, dust, and smoke.

They were five feet from the cab when a disheveled blonde woman fought her way from behind a deployed airbag and into the road. Gravity and shock grabbed the woman and threw her to the ground. She grabbed her bleeding head, stood, and, upon seeing the men in uniform before her, began screaming.

"Dead! They're all dead!"

"Ma'am, are you okay?" Agent Andrews asked as he holstered his pistol.

"They're all dead! All of them!" Megan continued.

"Ma'am, you've been in an accident," Agent Carter stated in a calm voice. "Agent Andrews is going to help you while I retrieve the first-aid kit from my vehicle."

Megan nodded. She paused for a moment then began yelling again at the sight of Agent Andrews moving toward her.

"No! We gotta leave. We gotta leave now. They'll kill us. They killed everyone."

"Who's everyone, ma'am?" Agent Andrews asked.

Agent Carter returned with a first-aid kit and a bottle of water. He held the bottle out to Megan. She grabbed the bottle, retreated a few steps, then chugged the container dry.

"You're in shock, ma'am," Agent Andrews informed Megan. "You need to sit down."

Megan slammed the empty plastic bottle to the ground and declared, "Screw that! We've...we've gotta go. I'm telling you, they killed everyone, and they'll kill us too."

"Who, ma'am?" Agent Carter inquired. "Who killed everyone?"

"These...these," Megan searched for the words. "These apes! Freakin' monkeys. Those monkeys killed everyone."

Agent Andrews and Agent Carter looked to one another then looked to Megan and offered in unison, "Chainsaws."

59.

"Light."

Hunter, Drake, and Dejah rushed to Taylor's side to get a better look at his promise.

"Light," Taylor repeated. "Up ahead."

Dejah smiled and clapped her hands. Hunter and Drake nodded in stoic understanding and fell back into position behind Taylor and Dejah.

Taylor led the group cautiously through the last ten yards of the tunnel and into a large cavern. All stared at the staircase of jumbled rock illuminated by a beam of light on the other side of the cave.

"Is that the way out?" Dejah asked.

Taylor nodded but the moment of hope was broken by the echoes of shrill barking from the tunnel they'd just exited.

Taylor, Hunter, and Drake instinctively checked their ammo and reported their findings to one another. Taylor put his hand to Dejah's back and commanded, "Go! Run!"

Dejah sprinted on bare feet across the cavern and toward the staircase. Hunter and Drake followed in haste. Taylor armed his last M84 grenade, threw it into the tunnel, and ran toward the far side of the cave. He counted the seconds then yelled, "Now!" and dropped to the cavern floor. Hunter and Drake did the same, taking Dejah with them.

Light and sound exploded from the tunnel and shook the cavern and all within it. Hunter stood and pulled Dejah to her feet. Drake stood and the three continued their sprint toward the way out.

Taylor stood and was immediately knocked to the ground. He rolled over and came up with his rifle at the ready. A bull baboon, its fur singed and smoky, caught the barrel of Taylor's rifle in his hands and threw it and Taylor aside with little effort.

Taylor fought to keep his footing, spun around, and fired a burst of   three   rounds. The first bullet struck the primate in the shoulder, the second into its trunk, and the third went wild. The beast howled in anger and charged. Taylor fired once more only to hear the click of an empty chamber. He unclipped the sling from his rifle and swung his weapon like a club into the advancing animal. The butt of the rifle crashed into the beast's lower jaw, sending a spray of blood and teeth outward. The animal collapsed in death and Taylor pulled his pistol.

"Taylor!" Hunter yelled across the cavern.

Taylor looked in Hunter's direction to see the warning on his face. Taylor turned back toward the tunnel to see a horde of primates spilling forth. Taylor drew a bead on the first animal with his pistol, dropped the animal with a single shot to the neck, then turned and ran toward the rock pile. Drake calmly walked from the rocks in Taylor's direction. She got into a crouch and waited for Taylor to pass her.

"Elon says hello!" Drake laughed and ignited her flamethrower, sending forth a hellish stream of flame exploding outwards of 50 feet. Primates at the lead of the troop burst into flames, their fur singed, their skin melted into their muscle. The troop howled in fear and surprise, shielded their eyes from the light and heat, and fought to breathe.

Taylor scrambled up the rock pile toward Hunter and immediately cupped his hands. Hunter stepped into his friend's cradle and Taylor launched him upward. Hunter grabbed the rim of the cave in and pulled himself up and onto the ledge. Hunter turned around, lay on his stomach, and plunged his hand into the hole. Taylor grabbed Dejah and lifted her up and toward Hunter. Dejah's fingers grasped Hunter's hand then grasped for anything as the rock jumble below her and Taylor shifted and collapsed.

Drake looked up from the base of the stack of rock and earth to see it fall upon her. She tried to run but was instantly buried by several thousand pounds from the waist down. The dust cloud from the collapse quickly dissipated and Drake looked through the haze to see a dozen primates descending upon her. She scrambled to free herself but knew the task hopeless given the weight upon her. She knew her legs were crushed and that her only hope was to free her sidearm so that she could end her life quickly.

She dug with bare hands through the rock and gravel, trying with all her might to get her Glock. She made it all the way through the rubble to the butt of the pistol before the primates circled above her and stared down at her with hungry eyes.

60.

Taylor stood from the rubble and coughed. He pulled Dejah to her feet, dusted her off, and asked, "Are you okay?"

Dejah began to speak and then screamed at the sight of Drake being pulled apart by a horde of primates below her. Taylor pulled Dejah to his waist and buried her face in his torso.

"We're safe," Taylor explained. "They won't come into the light and we're right here in the middle of it."

Dejah pulled from Taylor to study the beam of light she stood within. The light shone through the large hole above and downward into a semicircular space perhaps some 20 feet in diameter.

"See," Taylor said, pointing below the small mound they stood upon to the edge of the light. "They like the dark. They don't like the light."

Taylor had no sooner explained such than the baboons began testing his theory.

The primates crashed into the light with their hands shielding their coal black eyes. They darted toward Taylor and Dejah then retreated in haste as if the light was a source of pain or sudden reprimand. Taylor saw this and knew their time in the safety of the sun was limited.

"Hunter!" Taylor called into his radio. "Come in!"

No answer.

The primates continued their testing.

They ran into the light then retreated quickly, each time seeing how close they could come to the two humans they so desperately wanted.

"Hunter!" Taylor called again.

No response.

The primates got braver, running up the mountain to within feet of Taylor and Dejah before screaming and turning tail out of the light.

Taylor ignored his radio and instead screamed upward and out of the hole above him.

"Hunter!"

Dejah shrieked as a monkey pushed toward her. Taylor put two pistol rounds into the beast and the momentum of the blast sent it backward and into a somersault down the hill. The remaining primates howled and shrilled in anger, hurling themselves into the light, now more determined than ever to take the two figures before them. Taylor emptied his pistol into the first two animals to approach, dropping them in their tracks. He dropped the empty magazine from his pistol then slammed home a fully loaded one.

Dejah sobbed and clung to Taylor. A long shadow passed over Taylor and he looked upward, half expecting to see a troop of baboons descending upon him. Instead, he saw the bright yellow arm of an excavator lowering into the hole. The primates seized the opportunity the lack of light provided and rushed forward. Taylor holstered his pistol and grabbed Dejah by the waist. He lifted her up and commanded she grab ahold of the hydraulics. She did and Taylor yelled over the howls and screams quickly surrounding him, "Climb!"

Dejah pulled herself up the arm and toward daylight. Taylor launched upward and grabbed the bottom of the arm's jackhammer drill. He pulled himself up then was jerked downward from the extra weight upon his leg. He ignored the pain of claws and teeth driving into his ankle and calf and pulled himself up and further onto the hydraulic arm.

The arm raised up and out of the hole, taking Dejah, Taylor, and the primate attached to him into the sunshine. Taylor pulled his pistol, shoved it point blank against the eye of the beast clinging to his lower leg, and fired. The back of the animal's head exploded outward, sending shards of skull and brain matter into the cave below.

Taylor looked to the cab of the excavator that had just been used to save his life and to his friend Hunter sitting within and smiled.

61.

Agent Andrew, Agent Carter, and Megan reached the outer gate of Robert Wilson's ranch after a grueling hour and a half walk. The original plan was for Agent Andrews and Agent Carter to drive Megan to the nearest Border Patrol Check Station for medical assistance and to file a proper report, but the damage Megan inflicted on their government vehicle was too great. This, combined with the fact that the radio in the SUV wasn't working and that no one's cell phone had service, prompted Agent Andrews to make the decision to walk to Robert Wilson's ranch for assistance.

"Wilson's a good guy," Agent Andrew's explained to Megan during the hike. "He'll be able to help us until we can meet up with the Border Patrol."

"'Cause y'all are doing such a great job of protecting me so far," Megan complained.

"Ma'am, it was you that ran into our vehicle," Agent Carter reminded her. "We'd have driven you to aid quite easily had that not happened."

"Excuse me for not driving as safe as I could have but I was a little shell-shocked from seeing all my friends ripped apart by an ass-load of deranged monkeys," Megan shot back.

Agent Andrews and Agent Carter looked to one another in disbelief then back to Megan and said in unison, "Chainsaws."

Megan stopped in her tracks, sighed in disbelief, and declared, "Those chainsaws were covered in fur and had tails."

Agent Andrews and Agent Carter looked to Megan in bewilderment and each silently surmised that she had received severe head trauma during her collision, as her description of fur-covered chainsaws made no sense whatsoever.

The three travelers reached the house of Robert Wilson and rang the door. A short, rotund Hispanic woman in a cleaning uniform answered the door.

"*Buenos dias,*" the lady smiled.

"*Buenos dias,*" Agent Andrews replied. "We are seeking the assistance of Robert Wilson."

The lady nodded and waved Agent Andrews, Agent Carter, and Megan into the home and to follow her. The cleaning lady led the three down a heavily appointed hallway to a large trophy room overflowing with taxidermied animals from the world over. Robert Wilson stood from a worn leather couch, placed his lit cigar in an ashtray, and crossed the room to greet his guest.

"Andrews. Carter. Good to see you," Robert exclaimed, holding out his hand to each. He turned his attention to Megan and her worn look. "My dear, what's happened to you? Wait. You're one of the... You're from that paleontology group, aren't you?"

"There's been an accident," Agent Andrews began.

Robert turned to the cleaning woman. "Juana, some water please." Juana nodded and left the room.

Megan's eyes followed the woman sent to get her a beverage then paused at a mount that sat upon a table-height wooden stand. She pointed at the creature in surprise and fear. She tried to speak but was unable.

Robert saw this and said, "You've picked out the one animal in here I didn't take."

Megan dropped her hand and wrestled with the emotions overtaking her.

"Is that a...baboon?" Agent Andrews asked.

"How old is that mount?" Agent Carter continued. "It's all cracked."

Robert walked to the display to admire the mount. Its fur was dried and yellow from age, the skin worn and cracked, and its eyes looked more like cheap marbles then a representation of actual life. Still, it was one of his favorites.

"My great grandfather shot that here on the ranch back in the 1800s," Robert proudly explained. "Mexicans called it a *mono nocturno*. Night ape. Said they live in caves under the river and come out at night to feed."

"I've never heard of such a thing," Agent Andrews admitted.

"I've heard tell my great grandfather was quite the jokester," Robert recalled. "I've always suspected this old mount was fabricated to help perpetuate some joke of his. I've never had it looked at by professionals or by anybody that could give me a better explanation. I don't wanna get actual proof that this thing's not real and that it's just an old hoax or something."

"They're real," Megan declared. "And there's more of them."

62.

Taylor and Hunter didn't spend time wondering about the construction camp or what the black cloud of buzzards circling above them found so appealing in the trees behind where they stood. They ignored and shielded Dejah's eyes from the blood-soaked earth they encountered and instead made their way to an old crew cab 4 x 4 truck, smashed the window, and hot-wired it to life

Hunter drove them through ranch scrubland, along paths worn through the vegetation by errant cattle, and along the muddy shores of the Rio Grande until they found an area where the river was shallow and narrow enough to cross. They skirted into Mexico through properties run with goats and pigs and cut their way through barbwire fences until they hit the highway and then to the goat ranch that served as the Acuña Cartel's base of operations for the construction of the tunnel.

They hit the bunkhouse first where Taylor and Hunter replenished their ammo and downed two beers apiece in record time. They showed Dejah the shower, gave her a change of clothes they took from Ruck's footlocker, and told the girl to make them work until they could procure others for her.

Taylor and Hunter locked Dejah in the building and made their way to the barn where they found the remains of what was once Miguel and Arturo and the hole one of them had apparently bashed through the wall. They entered this and cautiously searched the barn to find only the dead remains of baboons and men eaten to the bone by such. They searched each room to find nothing but death until they came to the door to Eduardo's office.

Taylor tried the knob and finding it locked banged the door and called inside. When no one answered after the second attempt, Hunter kicked the door open to find it barricaded somehow on the inside. Taylor and Hunter pushed their way in to discover a weak and weary Eduardo hiding in the corner next to a safe. Eduardo stood and rushed to Hunter sobbing, "Thank God! Thank God!"

Hunter pushed Eduardo down to his office chair and explained the situation.

"My team's dead. All of them."

Eduardo sobbed into his hands.

"And as for here," Hunter continued, "you're it. The only one left."

"I tried to help," Eduardo tried to convince himself through the hands at his face. "I mean… I wanted to help… I—"

"You're going to help us right now if you want to live," Hunter instructed.

Eduardo's hands dropped and his head jutted upward.

"Anything," Eduardo promised. "Anything. Just get me out of here and away from all of this."

Hunter let his rifle drop to his side and drew his Glock.

"The Cartel's gonna pay for our pain and suffering. Put two million in each of our accounts," Hunter insisted. "Now."

"What?" Eduardo said, seriously taken aback.

Hunter pushed his pistol to Eduardo's temple. "I'm not a man used to having to explain myself. Two million in each of our accounts. Now."

"Yes…yes…yes, sir. I'll do it. No problems," Eduardo promised. "I'll… I can even… I'll even make it to where…where…"

"Where what?" Hunter prompted.

"I'll make it look like…department payments for an assignment. Materials. Payroll, etc."

"Now you're thinking," Hunter chided. "Crazy how inspiring a pistol to the head can be."

Taylor cracked a small smile at the comment.

Eduardo stammered through explanation after explanation of how and from where he was transferring the money. After several minutes of work, he had Hunter and Taylor check their respective accounts to see that each was two million dollars richer.

"How much cash we have on the premises?" Hunter continued.

"Which currency?" Eduardo asked.

"Don't get technical on me," Hunter barked.

"One hundred thousand U.S. Maybe 10,000 pesos."

"Good. We'll need that as well."

"I don't need the pesos," Taylor said. "I don't plan on hanging around in Mexico much longer."

"Agreed. The country's kinda worn out his welcome for me as well," Hunter added. He turned to Eduardo and said, "U.S. cash only."

Eduardo nodded and pulled the bundled cash from the safe in the corner he had hid behind. Hunter took the money. He put half in his vest and gave the other half to Taylor who did the same.

"Let's go," Hunter said, waving his pistol at Eduardo.

"Go…go where?" Eduardo stammered. "Are we leaving?"

"No. I'm putting you in that tunnel," Hunter stated.

"No…no…" Eduardo begged. "I did what you asked."

"You did," Hunter agreed. "But if I let you live, you'll tell your higher-ups just that."

"I won't… I won't tell anyone. I swear!" Eduardo pleaded.

"I know you won't." Hunter smiled. "Those monkeys will make sure of it."

63.

Taylor and Hunter returned to the bunkhouse to find Dejah asleep on Drake's bed. Taylor took a minute to relish in the child's peaceful sleep. He wondered how she could find such comfort so easily considering all that she had witnessed in the past few days.

Maybe it was pure exhaustion.

Maybe she was resilient.

Either way, Taylor mused, she'd need help dealing with all that had happened to her. Taylor had seen many men, with far stronger wills, fail to do such and the price they paid for it.

"Can't keep her," Hunter jokingly whispered. "She's got a family out there somewhere."

"I know," Taylor agreed.

"So, what you wanna do with her?" Hunter asked. "Leave her here? Drop her on some rich family's doorstep?"

"She's a dog now?" Taylor questioned.

"Wait. You can do that with dogs too?" Hunter laughed. "Just leave them someplace? I thought it was just kids you could do that with."

Taylor smiled at his friend's kidding then explained his plan. He'd find the girl's family in the United States, tell them everything he knew and everything that had transpired, and leave them some money with the instruction that Dejah would need counseling.

A lot of counseling.

"Then what?" Hunter asked.

"Find a beach. Start drinking my way through two million dollars."

"Sounds like a plan. Think I'll join you for a time."

"For a time?"

"I'm not done with this way of life. Neither are you. It's all we know."

Taylor and Hunter's planning was interrupted by stirring on Dejah's part. She twisted and writhed then shot up and gasped. She saw Taylor and Hunter looking down on her and realized she was safe and offered, "I had a bad dream."

Taylor sat next to her on the bed, stroked her hair, and said, "It's over now. The bad dream's over."

ABOUT THE AUTHOR

"If you mixed Ernest Hemingway, Robert Ruark, Hunter S. Thompson, and four shots of tequila in a blender, a 'Gayne Young' is what you'd call the drink!" – Author Doug Howlett

Gayne C. Young is the former Editor-in-Chief of North American Hunter and North American Fisherman - both part of CBS Sports -and a columnist for and feature contributor to Sporting Classics magazine. His work has appeared in magazines such as Outdoor Life, Petersen's Hunting, Texas Sporting Journal, Sports Afield, Gray's Sporting Journal, Under Wild Skies, Hunter's Horn, Spearfishing, and many others. He is the author of Bug Hunt, Teddy Roosevelt: Sasquatch Hunter, Vikings: The Bigfoot Saga, Bigfoot, The Boggy Creek Narratives, And Monkeys Threw Crap At Me: Adventures In Hunting, Fishing, And Writing, and numerous other titles. His screenplay, Eaters Of Men was optioned in 2010 by the Academy Award winning production company of Kopelson Entertainment.

In January 2011, Gayne C. Young became the first American outdoor writer to interview Russian Prime Minister, and former Russian President, Vladimir Putin.

CHECK OUT OTHER GREAT CRYPTID NOVELS

RETURN TO DYATLOV PASS
by J.H. Moncrieff

In 1959, nine Russian students set off on a skiing expedition in the Ural Mountains. Their mutilated bodies were discovered weeks later. Their bizarre and unexplained deaths are one of the most enduring true mysteries of our time. Nearly sixty years later, podcast host Nat McPherson ventures into the same mountains with her team, determined to finally solve the mystery of the Dyatlov Pass incident. Her plans are thwarted on the first night, when two trackers from her group are brutally slaughtered. The team's guide, a superstitious man from a neighboring village, blames the killings on yetis, but no one believes him. As members of Nat's team die one by one, she must figure out if there's a murderer in their midst—or something even worse—before history repeats itself and her group becomes another casualty of the infamous Dead Mountain.

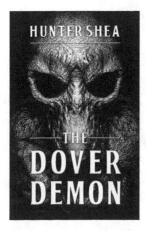

DOVER DEMON
by Hunter Shea

The Dover Demon is real...and it has returned. In 1977, Sam Brogna and his friends came upon a terrifying, alien creature on a deserted country road. What they witnessed was so bizarre, so chilling, they swore their silence. But their lives were changed forever. Decades later, the town of Dover has been hit by a massive blizzard. Sam's son, Nicky, is drawn to search for the infamous cryptid, only to disappear into the bowels of a secret underground lair. The Dover Demon is far deadlier than anyone could have believed. And there are many of them. Can Sam and his reunited friends rescue Nicky and battle a race of creatures so powerful, so sinister, that history itself has been shaped by their secretive presence?

CHECK OUT OTHER GREAT BIGFOOT NOVELS

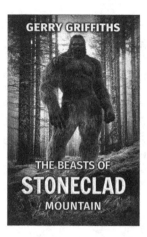

THE BEASTS OF STONECLAD MOUNTAIN
by **Gerry Griffiths**

Clay Morgan is overjoyed when he is offered a place to live in a remote wilderness at the base of a notorious mountain. Locals say there are Bigfoot living high up in the dense mountainous forest. Clay is skeptic at first and thinks it's nothing more than tall tales.

But soon Clay becomes a believer when giant creatures invade his new home and snatch his baby boy, Casey.

Now, Clay and his wife, Mia, must rescue their son with the help of Clay's uncle and his dog, a journey up the foreboding mountain that will take them into an unimaginable world...straight into hell!

BIGFOOT AWAKENED
by **Alex Laybourne**

A weekend away with friends was supposed to be fun. One last chance for Jamie to blow off some steam before she leaves for college, but when the group make a wrong turn, fun is the last thing they find.

From the moment they pass through a small rural town they are being hunted by whatever abominations live in the woods.

Yet, as the beasts attack and the truth is revealed, they learn that despite everything, man still remains the most terrifying evil of them all.